ROPE ME, COWBOYS

Coyote Ranch, Book One

ALEXA B. JAMES

First Edition

Published in the United States by Alexa B. James and Speak Now.

ISBN: 978-1-945780-21-9

Cover design by Ally Hastings of Starcrossed Covers.

For Gabe, whose love for Wyoming never wavers.

Chapter One

AMBER

One Week Before

"MAKE IT IRISH?" Haley whispered, nudging the table cloth back to reveal a silver flask at the hem of her sinfully short skirt.

"I wish," I hissed back. "I promised Mom I'd be on my best behavior."

"Since when does Amber Durant follow her mommy's orders?" asked Haley's brother, leaning forward to give me his most charming, douche-baggy smile.

"Since I haven't seen her all summer?" I said. "I'd like to hang out with her before she jets off to Africa and pretends to save starving children while really pushing a questionable pharmaceutical brand that hasn't gotten FDA approval."

Mark leered at me, taking in the scant cleavage allowed by my mother-approved wardrobe—a pink silk blouse that brought out my summer's end tan and a knee-length brown skirt. "When you give up on that and get schnockered, I'd be happy to give you some attention," he said.

"But make sure it's after midnight and no one sees you come in. I don't want my parents lecturing me about the company I keep."

"I have a boyfriend, remember?"

"Hmm, and yet, I don't see him offering to help you scratch that itch."

"He's sick," I said in my frostiest voice.

"Mark, seriously, shut up," Haley said, holding up a hand to block him from my view. Her parents had been lecturing her about the company she kept for years, but since she was no more "respectable" than me, they'd pretty well given up on her. They had decided to put all their eggs in the more promising, Mark-sized basket instead.

Haley turned in her seat, angling her shoulder away from Mark, and gave me her impish smile. "Are you sure you're okay? I've never known you to refuse a drink." With her short and curvy figure, fair skin and black pixie cut, she looked like a charming fairy god-sister offering up whiskey instead of pumpkins.

"I'm kind of nervous," I admitted. "Mom's been acting weird all day. She's been all…dreamy and smiley."

"She probably just got a new prescription," Haley assured me with a roll of her eyes.

"She said she has *an announcement*."

"That she's running for New York Senate again next fall, which everyone already knows?"

"Yeah, you're right," I said, trying to relax. I hated these stuffy formal parties, but it was nice to know I wasn't alone. Haley had been my best friend since elementary school, when we bonded over our mutual love of Circus Peanuts, our respective mothers' suckiness, and our tendency to misbehave at the private school we'd both attended, along with Mark and nearly every Manhattan politician's children. Since graduating earlier this year,

Haley and I had spent nearly every minute together. We planned to travel the world together before deciding if we could stomach four years of college.

"Maybe," I muttered, catching my mother's stern smile. She dabbed her mouth with a linen napkin and tapped at her wine glass with a fork, making a tinkling sound. The fifty or so politicos and schmoozers at the party stopped wheeling and dealing for two seconds and looked up.

"I—we—have an announcement," Mom said, standing and smoothing her Prada skirt over her trim hips. To keep her figure, she spent more time on the treadmill than she spent lecturing me about decorum. But I'd actually missed her during the summer, and I was determined to make amends now that I was an adult and no longer in high school. After all, one day I wanted to have a career. I couldn't blame her for putting that before her family.

"As you know, we spent the summer helping children in Africa gain access to much-needed medical supplies," she said, smiling at her philanthropist senator friend. "But we also fell in love."

I coughed out water, spewing it across my lobster thermidor.

Mom cast one warning glare at me before turning her attention to her audience. She smiled as far as her Botox would allow, and Senator Westling stood and put an arm around her. The gesture was so stiff it made my own shoulders cringe up towards my ears.

This must be a political move. My mother did not fall in love. She fell into Xanax-and-gin stupors. She fell into every new fad diet that took the talk shows by storm. If she fell in love with anything, it was the season's latest Armani-for-the-office collection.

"And we got married," she said.

I swayed slightly in my seat. Not that I expected to be first to know if she wanted to date again after Dad—she'd probably ask her political advisor before making that decision—but *married?*

"Like I said, if you need to drown your sorrows later tonight…" Mark said.

He was only a year older than us, but he already looked like a smarmy politician. I'd had a crush on him once, but after experiencing his douche-baggery firsthand, I stayed far away from his panty-melting smile. Behind it, his brain was full of sociopathic schemes.

Pretty much the norm for Manhattan private school boys bound for senatorial races. I was the luckiest girl alive to have found Charlie, the rare exception to the rule.

"Always the opportunist," Mark said with a shrug, turning back to his lobster.

It struck me that I should have been the one to say that, but I thought it as if from a distance. My brain seemed to be short-circuiting as my mother smiled wanly and described their 'charming little wedding among the villagers.'

She'd gotten married. And not only hadn't she invited me to be a bridesmaid, she hadn't invited me at all. Hell, she hadn't even told me!

"I think I'm going to need that Irishness after all," I said, picking up my glass and lowering it beside my chair. I wasn't about to call Mom out for forgetting me. It wasn't like I'd wanted to go to her stupid wedding anyway.

If I said something to her, she'd tell me I was being silly and selfish. And I was. I knew I was overreacting. I wanted my mom to be happy.

"I can't believe she didn't tell you," Haley said, her big brown eyes widening. "What a selfish bitch."

I could have kissed her for saying that. Instead, I took a

gulp of the whiskey, which burned like fire going down. "You're a life saver," I said, squeezing her arm. We'd saved each other from a lot through the years—bad dates, absentee parents, mean girls, creepy teachers, boring dinners…and parties. If there was one thing we'd learned in high school, it was how to party.

"Come on," I said, liquid courage warming my veins. "There's a band playing. Let's dance."

"That's the Amber I know and love," Mark said, though he'd never make a fool of himself by dancing in a restaurant to the string band that was playing. But I needed something to take the edge off my hurt, and it wasn't like I'd get arrested for dancing to elevator music.

Chapter Two

AMBER

Now

I SQUIRMED in my airplane seat, trying to get comfortable, but it was impossible. Giving up, I laid my head back and closed my eyes, trying to ignore the kid beside me who was flying a tiny toy airplane around in circles and making *vrooming* noises. My life was officially ruined. Instead of flying off on a whirlwind adventure with my best friend, I was being shipped off to babysit three spoiled stepbrothers I'd never met.

"Hey," the boy said loudly, pushing my arm off the armrest. I leaned against the window as he used the armrest for a runway for his toy plane.

I knew nothing about Senator Westling's kids except that they didn't live with him, so I was assuming they lived with their mother. I was going to have to be their nanny and "bond" with them, far away from reporters for *Page Six* and other gossip columns. Apparently, they'd had fun taking pictures of me running around town misbehaving the night of the announcement. Mom said a senator's daughter should be volunteering for community service, not showing everyone in a bar that I could put my leg behind my head.

Okay, so maybe she had a point.

Giving up on sleeping, I scrolled through my phone, tearing up through my laughter when I saw all the pictures of me and Haley having fun over the summer. I couldn't believe how fast our plans had fallen apart. Granted, I had made some questionable decisions on the night of my mother's wedding announcement. So I really couldn't blame her for wanting to hide me away in the middle of nowhere. Or Wyoming, to be exact.

The kid beside me shoved his finger so far up his nose I was afraid he was going to give himself brain damage. Wincing, I turned away and tried to ignore him.

I went back to my pictures. Over the past few days, I'd meticulously combed through my phone, erasing every picture of Charlie. If only I could erase him from my mind.

That was part of why I'd agreed to this three-month hiatus from real life. I didn't want to be around anything that reminded me of Charlie. I could have said no to my mom, moved out, and gotten my own apartment. I was eighteen, after all. But in truth, I felt like shit for embarrassing her in the media, and I wanted to make it up to her. If she loved this Westling guy, and these kids were going to be my brothers, then I might as well get to know them. They couldn't be worse than my seatmate, and I'd survived him for a good three hours now.

There was another reason I'd agreed to this trip. If I kept my head down, stayed out of trouble, and worked hard, Mom was going to fund my trip abroad in the spring. I'd promised Haley I'd do whatever it took. We would have those memories to look back on for the rest of our lives, and I would be across the world from Charlie, forgetting his shit-eating grin ever existed. I was determined to make that happen. If babysitting three nose-pickers would convince my mother I could be a responsible human being, then I'd do it. It was only three months. How bad could it be?

Chapter Three

AMBER

One Week Before

"I CAN'T BELIEVE your mom kicked us out." Haley howled with laughter as we strutted down the street. She clung to my arm, though we were both stumbling a bit by that point.

"Um, I can," I said. "We were moshing to a string quartet."

"Oh, man, you're right," Haley said, wiping away tears of laughter. "So what now, baby-girl? We gotta celebrate you getting a new daddy."

"Do *not* call him that," I said, bumping her so hard we nearly toppled into the street.

"You want to hit the clubs?" Haley asked. "I got my ID."

Our IDs were, of course, fake. A friend of Mark's had made a killing selling them to all the kids at our school. I had to admit, they were top quality.

"I don't feel like it," I said. "Can we just go to your house and binge-watch *Game of Thrones*?"

"Oh no," she said, pulling up short. "That's wallowing."

"I think this calls for wallowing."

"You only get to wallow for one night. Are you sure you want to use it already?"

"Yes."

"Tell you what," she said, taking my arm again. "Let's stop by that little sushi joint and get a vat of the miso soup you love so much, and if you still don't feel like forgetting your sorrows, then we'll go home."

"Deal," I said. "We can run by Charlie's on the way and bring him some. He sounded awful on the phone today."

I still had no idea how I'd landed a guy like Charlie. Not that there *were* other guys like Charlie. He was literally perfect in every way—handsome, athletic, class president, valedictorian, and hopelessly devoted. Haley's explanation was that I was badass. Mark's was that Charlie had a weakness for bad girls. This was obviously not a flaw in my eyes, since I was the bad girl he had a weakness for.

The one area we didn't agree on was his vow to wait until marriage to have sex, and it wasn't like I could fault him for that. The problem was, we were only eighteen and that was a long-ass wait. But I knew I'd never find a guy like him if I spent the next twenty years searching. I made due with the finger vibrator Haley had given me for Christmas two years earlier when I'd told her about Charlie's vow of celibacy. She'd also bought me a package of rechargeable batteries so I wouldn't blow my college fund on batteries. Haley was nothing if not thoughtful.

"Of course," she said. "Come on, let's get a cab."

I felt a little guilty for running by my boyfriend's place when I was spending time with Haley, but she wouldn't fault me for it. She knew I'd never ditch her to hang out with a guy, even Charlie. And she loved Charlie because he loved me. If I were sick, he'd check in on me, probably bringing chocolate, homework, cold medicine, and chicken soup. If it weren't for his cold, he'd have been there for moral support tonight just like she was. Plus, my mother loved him, so she always forgave my bad behavior a little when he was around. The least I could do in return was make a quick stop for miso soup delivery on my way to Haley's.

When the cab finally pulled up in front of his Park Avenue apartment, we piled out, giggling and trying to hold the takeout bag upright so the soup didn't spill. We told the cab driver to wait, and I let myself in. Charlie had gotten his own place after graduation, and I had my very own key. I still felt a little thrill of pride every time I used it.

The apartment had been decorated by one of the best in the business, and as always, it was immaculate. I expected to find Charlie wrapped in a blanket on the couch watching TV, but the spacious living area was empty.

"He must be sleeping," I whispered, tiptoeing towards his bedroom.

"Is he watching porn?" Haley asked, stifling a giggle.

"Charlie doesn't watch porn," I said, rolling my eyes. And then I heard what she must have already heard. A breathy, gasping sound. My tipsy brain couldn't come up with an alternative to the porn explanation, but I was sure it was something totally innocent. It was Charlie, for God's sake. The guy wore sweater vests.

Because I knew it wasn't anything he wouldn't want me to see, I marched my drunk ass right into his bedroom without even knocking.

And then I screamed.

As I had so confidently assured my bestie, Charlie was not watching porn. If there had been a camera set up, however, he could have been starring in porn. Hell, maybe there was. I didn't have the presence of mind to look around his familiar, tastefully decorated bedroom. I was too busy staring at my boyfriend.

He was lying on his back, halfway off the bed, with a naked brunette kneeling between his knees, her head bobbing as she devoured his previously-unseen-by-me cock. A naked redhead straddled his face, moaning in rhythm with the strokes of his tongue. Apparently, he had no reservations about oral sex before marriage. Or three-somes, as long as there was no penetration—or girlfriends—involved.

When I screamed, the brunette didn't even seem to notice. She was too engrossed in blowing my boyfriend.

The redhead twisted around and looked down at Charlie's face—the part of it that wasn't buried in her twat. "Oh, is your girlfriend?" she asked.

Charlie pulled his mouth from her pussy long enough to peer around her ass at me. He gave me a shit-eating grin and released the girl's thigh to make a welcoming motion that included me *and* Haley.

"Come join us," he said. "Or should I say, join us and come?"

"You—you piece of shit," I screeched, wincing at my shrill tone even as it came from my mouth.

"Four mouths are better than two," he said with a wink, then buried his face in the redhead's crotch.

"Give me that," Haley said, snatching the forgotten takeout bag from my hand. She popped the lid off one of the tall soup careens and pushed it into my hand while she opened the second one.

"On the count of three," I said, and together we doused perfect Charlie with two quarts of scalding miso soup.

Chapter Four

AMBER

Now

I STUMBLED off the tiny plane that had flown me the last leg of the trip. The turbulence had been so bad I thought I might get sick. The nausea had passed but now my legs felt rubbery, and I was a little dizzy as I descended the shaky ladder towards the ground. It definitely did not feel sturdy enough to hold the guy who was waiting to come down after me, and I was fairly certain it hadn't passed FSA inspections.

I exhaled in relief when I made it to the ground. A gust of October wind swept across the tarmac, bringing with it a dry chill that felt somehow wild and spooky. I shivered as I wheeled my suitcase across the tarmac towards the glow of the airport, which was really just a hangar. The night around us was so…black. Beyond the airport, I could see everything and nothing at once. No tall buildings obscured the view, but then, no lights lit it up, either. There were a few small buildings, and houses in the distance.

The air smelled so clean and fresh that I kept inhaling

until I got even more dizzy. I stopped myself, because I really didn't want to pass out on the expensive shoes of my mother's new husband's old wife.

Gripping the handle of my suitcase as another gust of dry, cold wind whistled across the tarmac, I hurried forward. Something about the place made me want to run, as if something were going to jump out of the dark and chase me.

Get it together, Am, I told myself. I wasn't seriously afraid of the dark. Except, it never really got dark in New York, so how would I know?

I reached the airport and went through, got the rest of my luggage, and pulled it outside. A single bench sat off to one side, but most of the airport appeared deserted. I glanced along the lane that ran in front of the building. The nosepicker was jumping up and down on the bumper of a minivan while his family loaded in suitcases. A little closer to me, a beat up old red pickup sat idling. And against that leaned the hottest guy I'd ever seen.

He gazed out into the night from beneath the brim of a cowboy hat. His dark lips moved slightly as he chewed on the end of a piece of dry grass. He was tan and tall, with broad, sculpted shoulders shown off to full advantage by a plaid shirt with the sleeves torn off. He'd left his shirt untucked above a pair of jeans that fit him oh-so-well and a pair of dusty cowboy boots.

Damn. If all the guys in Wyoming looked this good, maybe the next three months wouldn't be so bad after all.

"Hey there," he said to me when he caught me checking him out. "Are you Amber?"

I gulped. "That's me. Are you picking me up? I mean, like, giving me a ride. I wasn't asking if you were trying to pick me up. Nope. Totally was not even thinking about that. Not even a little."

He laughed and strode over, thrusting out a work-worn hand. When it closed around mine, it felt like it could pulverize my bones if it wanted. Luckily, he was only after a handshake, not bone-meal. He gave my hand a tight squeeze, which, ridiculously, made my legs a little more quivery than they already were. "I'm Sawyer," he said with a grin. "And I'm here to pick you up."

I couldn't help but smile back. "Awesome," I breathed.

"If you'll just unhand me, I'll get your bags."

"Oh! Right. Yeah, sorry about that. It was the plane ride. I blame that. Seriously. It was long." I dropped his hand and continued to ramble as he picked up my bags, as promised, and swung them over the side of the truck bed and settled them in. I watched his muscles flex as he lifted them. They were really, really nice muscles. He must spend hours in the gym, I thought as I headed for the passenger door.

He slid in front of me and pulled it open, holding it for me until I'd climbed in before closing it gently behind me. He patted the hood of the truck like it was a beloved horse as he circled it before climbing into his seat.

"You all ready?" he asked. "Buckle up, Princess. It's gonna be a long one."

"Oh boy. I like the sound of that."

He shot me a surprised grin as he laid his arm across the back of the seat and twisted around to see behind him as he backed up. I didn't know this guy from Ted Bundy, but I was kinda disappointed when he didn't oh-so-casually drape his arm around me afterwards.

Instead, he dropped his hand to the radio and dialed across the stations as he pulled away from the airport.

It was totally the rebound thing. I'd just been dumped in the worst way. Of course I was lusting after this sexy, sexy cowboy.

"What kind of music do you like?" he asked as we edged away from the few businesses and out of town.

"Oh, all kinds," I said, marveling at how far apart the houses were. There were entire blocks of darkness between them!

"We might as well start getting to know each other," he said. "It's our job to keep you out of trouble for the next three months. I guess that starts with knowing what kind of bar you're likely to run off to."

"What?" I squealed, turning to him. "You live with Mrs. Westling? Are you, like, her ranch hand or something? She does live at the ranch, right? Because I didn't get the full scoop from my mom and Senator Westling, but they did tell me that much. And that, you know, I was an embarrassment to their family name, and I had to go babysit his kids until I learned to make better decisions. Wait, oh my god, you're not her new husband, are you? Because if you are, I'm just going to come out and say it, she totally won the divorce. Not that my mom isn't pretty, because she totally is, but Mrs. Westling must be a real cougar. That's all I'm saying."

"Is that really all you're saying?" He grinned sideways at me as we sped along a straight road that disappeared into…nothing. It stretched on as far as I could see, without a single car in sight. Suddenly, I felt as if we were hurtling through space. I gripped the dash and stared straight ahead.

"Sorry," I muttered, sinking down in my seat, my face warming. "I talk a lot when I get nervous. It's better than sweating, though, right?" I winced that I'd put that lovely image into his head and vowed to shut the hell up. Otherwise, I'd have told him my entire life story before he dropped me off and disappeared into the night forever.

But apparently, that wasn't happening. Apparently, I was going to see a lot of this guy.

I wished I wasn't quite so excited about the prospect.

"To answer your question," he said with a slight drawl. "I'm not married to Mrs. Westling, or anyone else. Actually, there is no Mrs. Westling. Our mother remarried a few years ago and took new name, and none of us are married."

"Us?" I said, suddenly feeling the unmistakable butterflies of premonition as his words sank in.

"That's right," he said. "Dad told you there were three of us, right?"

"You're the snot-nosed kid I'm supposed to babysit?"

Sawyer laughed. "I guess so."

"And you all live on the ranch?"

"Yup."

"And I guess they're all grown up, too?" I squeaked.

"All grown up," he agreed with a grin in my direction.

I was in so much trouble.

Chapter Five

AMBER

One Week Before

"I'M STAGING AN INTERVENTION," Haley said as we hurried to the cab. "This is too big for wallowing at home, and we're out of miso soup. We're going out dancing."

"I look like I'm going to a fundraiser."

"You look hot," Haley said. "Unbutton a few buttons, and you'll give off a sexy librarian vibe."

"At least he had the decency not to say *it's not what you think.*"

"His dick was literally still in that bitch's mouth," Haley said, slamming the cab door behind us. "How could it not be what you think?"

"*Four mouths are better than two,*" I raged. "I barely passed math and even I could count five people in that room."

"Maybe he forgot about the girl sucking his dick."

"Maybe he wasn't counting *me*," I said, my voice cracking. "He obviously doesn't want to have sex with me, or he already would have. Waiting until marriage, my ass."

What really hurt was that he'd had no reason to cheat.

I'd have done all that with him. I'd *wanted* to do all that. But noooo. Charlie had wanted to "preserve my chastity."

And for three years I'd let him, missing out when all my friends got laid, listening to Haley's horrible and hilarious sex stories, while I pretended I didn't mind that my boyfriend didn't want to go beyond kissing with me. I'd respected his beliefs. But it turned out, his beliefs were bullshit. He wanted sex, too, he just didn't want me.

"Shut up," Haley said, her nails digging into my forearm. "This is absolutely in no way your fault."

"You're right," I said, allowing rage to replace the shattered feeling inside me. "It's not like I was the one holding out so he had to get it elsewhere."

"And even if you were holding out, there's no excuse for cheating," she said fiercely. "Besides, did you see his dick? That thing was not very impressive. No offense, but I think you dodged a bullet right there."

"It did kind of look like a bullet, didn't it?"

"That's better," Haley said. "Now. We're going to go out dancing, and loads of guys are going to want you, because you're amazing. And I'm going to buy you so many shots you puke, and take care of you all the way home."

"I'm not going home," I said. "I've been waiting to have sex for three years, and now I don't have a reason not to. I'm going to get laid tonight."

Chapter Six

AMBER

Now

IT WAS after midnight when we pulled up at the ranch. I had passed the last hour in a semi-conscious state, somewhere between awake and asleep. It was so dark here that it was hard to see anything out the windows, and I was tired after flying across the country.

Finally, the truck stopped and Sawyer threw it into park. "You awake?" he asked, giving me a gentle shake. Heat sank into my shoulder from his touch, and I had to resist the urge to sleepily crawl into his lap and curl up there.

"Let's get you inside," he said with a smile. "You look like you could use a good night's rest."

"Thanks," I said, smiling through a yawn. "If you'll just show me where to sleep, I'll grab my bags and crash. I'm beat."

"I'll bring your bags up," Sawyer said. "Don't worry about a thing."

With that, he hopped out of the truck. A whistling

wind slammed his door for him. As I climbed out, the wind tore at me like a wild animal. There were no buildings to block the wind here. A big lodge loomed over the drive, but it was dark inside, and I couldn't make out much detail.

"Go on in," Sawyer called from the back, where he was unloading my bags.

When I turned towards the house, a giant loomed out of the darkness at me.

I screamed.

"Whoa, Nelly," he said in a soft voice.

I almost screamed again when a huge paw reached out for me.

"Don't go scaring the girl," Sawyer said, coming around with two of my bags.

"Sorry," said the giant. He switched on a headlamp, which pretty well blinded me. I threw up a hand to shield my eyes.

"You know this guy?" I asked, huddling against Sawyer.

"This is Holden," he said. "He's my—our—brother."

"Pleasure to meet you," Holden said, holding out a hand.

Awkwardly, I took it. His huge, hot hand engulfed mine, firm but gentle, and a feeling of comfort immediately settled my nerves. Instead of snapping at him, my words came out teasing. "Well, Holden, you should really think twice about sneaking up on girls in the dark. You're lucky I didn't have out my pepper spray. That would probably not have fostered the warm and cozy feelings our parents are aiming for."

"Probably not," Sawyer agreed with an easy smile.

"I apologize," Holden rumbled, holding out an arm like he was going to escort me to a royal ball. "Can I make it up to you by welcoming you to the Coyote Ranch?"

"You may," I said, slipping my hand into the crook of his elbow. Let me just say, if Sawyer's muscles were nice, this guy's were world-class. He could do some serious damage if he ever decided to punch someone. A cheating, pussy-eating ex-boyfriend, for instance.

We climbed the wooden steps and crossed the wooden porch. I felt like a dainty fairy next to the giant as we stepped inside a large room with polished hardwood floors, rough wooden walls, and high ceilings with exposed wooden beams. A fireplace glowed gently at one side of the room, topped by an empty mantel and a rack of antlers. Three leather chairs and a matching sofa formed a semi-circle around a bearskin rug in front of the fireplace. Otherwise, the room was bare, making it feel cavernous rather than cozy.

"Your room is upstairs," he said, nodding at a set of stairs set against the far wall. He led me up the wide wooden staircase that turned at a sharp angle before reaching the second floor. A long railing stretched along one side of the landing, which looked over the main floor of the lodge below. Holden led me along the hall to the last room, which he opened to usher me inside. The large room was warm and spacious and obviously empty. Like the rest of the house, it had no decorations and showed no personality.

"Is this mine?" I asked, turning around in the empty space at the bottom of the king bed. A bathroom door stood open to one side, a huge closet to the other. "Did you give me the master suite?"

Holden cleared his throat and scuffed his toe against the floor. "You're the only girl," he said in his deep, soft voice. "We figured you'd be more comfortable having your own bathroom."

Maybe it was the lack of sleep, or the huge upheaval in

my life, but suddenly, emotion choked up my throat. I had to stop myself from throwing my arms around this soft-spoken giant. In truth, I kind of wanted to, if only to see what a mountain of solid muscle would actually feel like. I wondered if he was as hard as he looked.

Naughty Am, I scolded myself. *This is your brother!*

I'd come out here to have a break from partying, to slow down and relax and enjoy the scenery…outside the house. But I couldn't help but look over Holden as he flicked the switches in the bathroom and closet, showing me everything in the room I'd be sleeping in for the next three months. He was huge, easily six-and-a-half feet tall, and equally big in every other way, with a massive chest, arms, and shoulders. His brown hair was cut short and neat, though he had sideburns and a shade more than five-o'clock shadow on his strong jaw.

"Make yourself at home," he said. His phone rang just then, and he checked it then slipped it back into his pocket without answering. "We don't have a lot of company, so if there's anything you're missing, just let us know, and we'll do our best to help you out."

"Thanks," I said, my eyes straying to the bed.

"This is your house now, too, so you don't have to ask to use anything or go anywhere. We got a couple hundred acres, so walk around and get acquainted with how it all works. Be careful of the electric fences, and don't wander onto the neighbor's property, but otherwise, you'll be fine here."

"Thank you," I said, emotion welling in my chest. Why was he being so nice? A guy had never even asked me to stay the night with him before, let alone given me free reign of his apartment. This guy was giving me the ranch.

"From what our dad said, I got the feeling you didn't

exactly come here willingly. But for what it's worth, I'm glad you came."

"Me, too," I said, avoiding his gentle brown eyes. I was afraid I'd start crying if he didn't quit giving me so much sympathy.

"Don't look so sad," he said, stepping closer and brushing my blond hair away from my cheek. "I'm glad you came to us to keep you out of trouble. I can't imagine how many temptations wait around every corner in a big city. But don't worry. No harm in the whole world will reach you here—not before it goes through the three of us."

If only he knew. The temptations in the city might be plenty, but here, I was dealing with a whole new kind of temptation.

Chapter Seven

SAWYER

Now

I COULD TELL by the silence at breakfast that Waylon hadn't gotten over his anger at our father for sending us a glorified babysitting job. Amber's confusion at the airport the night before replayed in my mind, and I smiled to myself as I tossed a dozen eggs into the spitting skillet on the woodstove. That made two people who thought this was a babysitting job.

Holden stepped inside, wiped his boots on the mat, and dumped a towering armload of wood into the wood box. "Frost is coming soon," he said, opening the door to feed the stove. Usually, we'd let it burn down when we went out to do chores, but all of us were thrown off by the presence of a woman in the house. It had been a long time since we had one of those.

I slid a pile of eggs onto each of our plates, and we all dug in.

"You gonna make me ask?" Waylon grumbled after a few minutes.

"What's to say?" I answered. "She'll be gone in three months."

"She's beautiful," Holden said, not looking up from his eggs.

"So she's just what Dad said she'd be," Waylon said, pushing his chair back. "A spoiled socialite. Whatever that is."

"She's a city girl," I said. "We knew that."

"And we're saddled with her because she can't get her shit together on her own."

"It's three months," I said. "She didn't murder someone. She just got a little wild. We've all done as much after a night of too many whiskeys."

"If Dad's happy, we should be happy," Holden said.

"Three months," Waylon said, rising from the table. "That's too damn long. Anything can happen in three months."

I wondered if he was thinking about Maria, and how quickly things had gone south after she'd moved in.

"Three months isn't much," Holden said, finishing up his eggs. "But it's an eternity."

We were probably all thinking about Maria, and the mess it had caused when she turned tail and ran. We were finally all back to good with each other, brothers until the end. We couldn't make the mistake of letting a woman come between us again, no matter what role she played in our lives.

After we washed up and stacked our plates in the drying rack with last night's dinner dishes, we headed out to do the morning chores.

I stopped Waylon at the barn door. "You okay, brother?" I asked. "I thought we talked it out and agreed on this. We can call Dad and tell him the deal's off if you aren't on board."

Waylon grunted. "I'm on board," he said. "We need that loan to save the ranch. That doesn't mean I gotta like it."

"Oh, you'll like her, all right," I said.

"If you give her a fair chance, that is," Holden added.

Waylon pushed past me with a scowl that would scare the cows up from the pasture. He opened the barn door and strode off towards the side-by-side, calling back over his shoulder as he went. "I have no intention of giving her a chance or liking her. She may be our stepsister forever, but she's only our problem for a few months."

I wasn't quite so sure.

Chapter Eight

AMBER

Now

WHEN I WOKE up the next morning, the house was so quiet I thought I'd gone deaf. I leapt out of bed, scrambling frantically for my phone. The tone when I turned it on told me I still had my hearing, and I faceplanted on the bed in relief. I wasn't deaf. Wyoming was just freakishly devoid of pissed off drivers blaring their horns.

After my heartbeat had returned to normal, I rolled over and sprawled out, luxuriating in the huge, soft bed. But soon enough, my stomach growled and I had to give up the warmth of the blankets. After freshening up and getting dressed, I headed downstairs. I hadn't heard a peep from the rest of the house, so I took my time looking over everything in the big lodge. The cursory glance I'd given it the night before proved to be enough, though. There wasn't much to see besides the building itself.

The lingering smell of food drew me to the kitchen. If I'd been hoping for a homemade breakfast waiting for me,

I was sorely disappointed. The fireplace was going in the big living room, and a small black stove was putting off heat in the kitchen, but there was not scrap of food sitting out. Besides a rack of dishes beside the sink, the kitchen was as barren as if no one lived there.

Luckily, the refrigerator was stocked with lots of food, and I happened to make a mean omelet. I whipped one up and scarfed it down, grateful no one was there to see me inhaling the food. After eating nothing but airplane food the night before, I was famished.

Having fortified myself with breakfast, I still hadn't seen any of my stepbrothers, but I remembered Holden's warm welcome the night before. A smile crept across my face and refused to leave when I thought of him filling up my bedroom with his genuine warmth and earnestness. He'd said that everything was mine to explore, and if I wasn't going to be stuck wiping snotty noses and nagging three kids to get off their phones and get outside all day, I was going to take full advantage. I couldn't believe how much I'd lucked out. Not only was I not watching spoiled kids all winter, I was living with two super hotties.

Who are your brothers, I reminded myself. Which was true in a weird legal sense. But there was no law against looking.

Grabbing a canvas jacket off the hook beside the door, I stepped outside. A blast of cold hit me first thing. It wasn't the kind of clinging cold we got in New York, where the snow stuck around for ages in the spring, sitting in grey slushy piles in the gutters and sticking to your boots. This was a dry chill, windy and wild. I pulled the jacket tighter around myself, although like the house, the clothes here were lacking in style.

But I didn't care any more than I would have if the

boys turned out to be five-year-olds like I expected. So, I headed down the steps and looked around. The ranch was flat as far as I could tell, but there was a gorgeous view of the mountains jutting up in one direction. In the other, at the edge of a seemingly endless expanse of fields, a line of trees had burst into bright, daffodil yellow.

"Yoo-hoo," a high voice called. I nearly jumped out of my skin. But I needed my skin for later use, so instead of jumping out of it entirely, I just jumped a foot into the air and shrieked.

"Oh, I didn't mean to scare you now," said a woman who looked to be in her late fifties or early sixties. She was short and round, with short, curly blue hair, narrow eyes, and round, red cheeks. As she waddled up to the porch, I checked for a vehicle, but she must have parked around back. Or she lived here.

"Hi," I said, bounding down the steps so she wouldn't have to walk up. She seemed a little out of breath already.

"Hi, there," she said. "I thought I saw one of the boys coming home late last night."

"You live here?" I asked, thinking she was the cook or housekeeper.

"Out back, in the last cabin," she said. "Who are you?"

"Oh, sorry," I said, holding out my hand. "I'm Amber. Their stepsister."

"Oh, *you're* Amber," she said, her beady little eyes scanning me up and down. "Hmph."

What was that supposed to mean? I drew myself up straight and tall. I wasn't going to let this nosy old bird intimidate me.

"And you are?" I asked, giving her my best New York attitude. Which, admittedly, wasn't great.

"Oh, I'm Mrs. Grimes," she said. "Mr. Grimes works

with the cattle, but I'm around here all day, and just next door every night."

I wasn't sure what she was insinuating, but I didn't like it one bit.

"Thanks," I said. "I'll make sure to come by if we need anything."

Just then, a man strode around the side of the house. He looked about the same age as her, but he had on a ball cap and a canvas jacket just like the one I'd pulled on.

"Oh, Gerald," Mrs. Grimes tootled. "Come and say hello to our new resident."

Gerald stopped and took me with one sweeping motion of his eyes. "Hiya," he said, nodding at me as he pulled on a pair of work gloves. "I got to get to work. Nice to meet you." And with that, he was gone.

"He keeps to himself," Mrs. Grimes said. "Likes to say that whatever happens under a man's roof is his own business. That's why we ladies have to stick together. Isn't that right?" She gave me a wink.

"I guess so," I said slowly.

"Good," she said. "You make sure to let me know if there's anything going on that I should know about."

"Okay."

"I work in the garden and clean up in the big house," she said. "They don't let me go into the cabins. Say they're private."

She looked like she was waiting for me to dish up some gossip, but I'd barely gotten out of bed. And I wouldn't be contradicting my stepbrothers, anyway. If they didn't want her snooping around, I certainly wasn't going to invite her in. Holden had told me I could go anywhere, but I didn't figure I should mention that to Mrs. Grimes.

Instead, I told her I was going out for a walk, and I left her in the driveway. Shaking off the odd encounter, I headed along a narrow dirt road that was nothing more than two tire tracks worn in the grass.

I was on a ranch. In Wyoming. A week ago, my life had been totally normal. Now I had to keep reminding myself it was real.

I almost squealed with delight when I saw my first cow. Wishing Haley was there to share the experience, I whipped out my phone and snapped a pic, but it was so far away that it didn't look much different from a dog. Sighing, I put my phone in the jacket pocket, absently fingering the gloves I found there. The thought of not sharing this moment with Haley made my eyes feel all salty. Suddenly, I missed her painfully. She would totally get me right now, and we'd forever laugh about the pic I sent her of real-life cow.

I had to get a picture. Pressing my lips together in determination, I stepped forward. The barbed wires of the fence were strung just close enough that I wasn't sure I could slip through. That was the one thing Holden had warned me about, so I figured it was pretty important. I walked along the fence a little way, trying to find a good spot. Further along, I saw a section where the wires were bent a little, making them about two feet apart instead of eighteen inches.

"Okay, Haley," I muttered under my breath. "I'm going in."

Preparation was key. I looked to see if anyone was around to stop me. Nope. I zipped the canvas jacket so the zipper wouldn't fall against the wire and electrocute me. I pulled on the gloves in case they would protect me from cow dung if I accidentally had to put a hand down for balance. I put up the jacket's hood so it wouldn't catch on the wire above me. And I dove the for opening.

Okay, I didn't really dive. I carefully bent and lifted one

leg, then put it back down, not sure I had good enough balance to slip through the wires not using my hands. Bent over like that, lifting one leg in the air, I probably looked like a dog stopping to pee on a bush in the park. Good thing there was no one around to see me.

Gathering my courage, I channeled my inner ballerina. It was all about balance. My mom had put me in dance classes for a few years, before it became clear that I was hopelessly uncoordinated and about as competitive as a cow.

A cow that I'm now going to take a picture of.

Slowly, I lifted one leg and extended it over the wire. Not too bad. I eased my body over and set my foot down. Now I had a hot barbed wire between my legs. But I had no intention of touching it, so it didn't matter one bit. I eased my body through, bending my knee and sliding my body sideways like a ninja master. I even remembered to duck my head.

When I lifted my other foot off the ground, though, my balance wobbled. Instead of trying to catch it, I dove sideways, through the fence, and landed in the grass. The wire was rippling from where my boot had hit it, but it either hadn't been long enough to convey a shock, or the thick soles of my boots had protected me.

Thanks to the resurgence of 90's fashion trends, my boot soles were probably thick enough to protect me from the shock of an electric chair. Which is probably where my mother would send me if I got kicked off Coyote Ranch on my first day for trespassing in a cow pasture.

Picking myself up, I examined the borrowed jacket, looking for signs of cow dung. I didn't see much on it but some bits of dry grass and dirt, though there was something suspect near my foot. It looked like a wrinkled, grey pancake, but I wasn't taking chances, so I skirted around it and headed for the cows.

Holy hellions, I'd done it! I'd navigated an electrocution device, and I was going to get a picture for my bestie. Wyoming was going to be awesome.

Chapter Nine

AMBER

One Week Before

MY HEAD WAS LYING next to a toilet. My mouth tasted like I might have drunk toilet water. My neck was cramped, my shoulder ached, and my whole body was stiff with cold from lying on a tile floor in just my underwear and bra.

I sat up. I had no idea where I was. This was bad, even for me. Sure, I liked to party and pretend to be a bad girl back in high school, but four whole months had passed since then. I was reformed. Or at least, I had learned to control my drinking. And I'd wanted to get laid, but this had not been part of the plan. I tried to cover myself with my hands, as if some perv might be watching me through a camera.

The truth was, I'd never been as bad as I pretended. I was a huge faker. I didn't do drugs, though I had to pretend to keep up my image. Sure, I liked a fruity cocktail, but who didn't? The things tasted like heaven, and who could resist those cute little umbrellas that looked like they belonged in Barbie's beach house?

Okay, so I wasn't perfect, but we all had to do what we could to survive high school. And despite my poor decision-making skills, I had always had Charlie there to deliver me safely home before dawn with nothing more than a chaste kiss. When I went out without him, Haley and I had a strict stick-together policy.

Stumbling to my feet, fear quaked through me. Where was Haley? Was she okay? Had we been drugged and kidnapped? Or worse? And where the hell were my clothes? I remembered telling her I was going to get laid, and I remembered arriving at a bar, and taking tequila shots, and dancing… I guessed from my state of undress that I'd succeeded in my mission, though like my infamous first attempt at getting laid, I had no memory of it.

I reached between my legs. My panties were dry, and I wasn't sore. A flash of memory jolted through my mind—Charlie looking up at me from the street. There was no way I'd let him out of this one, even to prove that I could give him what those girls had. Or had I? And where the hell was I?

Groping the walls, I stumbled from the bathroom into a hallway with abstract art prints on the wall and heavy, Oriental rugs that did not match the paintings at all. "Haley?" I whispered. Clearing my throat, I called again. "Haley!"

"Miss Durant," said a disapproving voice behind me. I turned to see a man in uniform—a servant. My hands flew to cover myself before I saw that he was holding a folded towel with my clothes laid over the top. "I've washed your things. Your mother requests your presence when you've cleaned yourself up."

My mother?

Nodding mutely, I grabbed the clothes and dashed into the bathroom, slamming the door behind me. This wasn't my mother's house, or her brownstone. So it must be… Senator Westling's. As I dressed, dread clung to my every move. Way to make an impression on my mom's new husband. Oh my god. Was I going to have to call him Dad?

And how the hell had I ended up at Senator Westling's? I didn't even know where he lived. No matter how drunk we'd been, we would have given the cab driver Haley's address and gone back there to pass out. What the hell had happened after the tequila shots?

I wracked my brain, but besides that image of Charlie's face, I drew only a blank.

Ten minutes later, after splashing my face and rubbing toothpaste over my teeth with my finger, I shuffled into the kitchen. Mom and Senator Westling were sitting at the table together, both on their devices. They looked up as one, both setting down their tablets when they saw me. For one weird moment, I thought they looked like parents about to discipline their naughty child.

And that's exactly what they did…or so they thought.

Chapter Ten

AMBER

Now

WYOMING TOTALLY SUCKED. I had done everything right. I snuck up to the cows, but they danced away from me, bumping each other with their big butts. Mooing and moaning, they cast baleful glances my way, as if I meant to shoot them with a gun instead of a cell phone camera.

"Stupid cows," muttered, stepping forward. Something slid under my foot and I shrieked, sure it was a rattlesnake. But no. It was one of the grey pancakes. The upper crust of it had slid off when I stepped on it, and my heel was now an inch deep in brownish-green cow dung. I didn't have to look up a picture to know what it was. It smelled like…well, like shit.

"Craptastic," I said. I spent a minute wiping my heel on any spots of grass I could find, though now I could see millions of the dung-patties, some of them still brown but most grey. I could hardly find any grass, and most of what I did find was brown.

At last, I took a few pictures for Haley, though they

weren't as close as I'd have liked. I wanted a close-up of a cow's soulful eyes and shiny wet nose. But they weren't giving me their good side today. Maybe they'd come around once I'd been here a few months.

Before I went home, I vowed to take a picture of the prodigious poopers. Then I headed back, not wanting any of the boys to come along and laugh at me for being grossed out by cow dung or not being able to get up close. They probably threw their legs over the cows and rode them all over the farm. I laughed to myself at the image of giant Holden sitting on a cow. It would probably collapse under his weight. I wondered how he'd even manage with a girl. He'd probably crush her with his weight, too.

Giggling a little, I made it back to the fence. Pulled my gloves back on, since I'd had to take them off to take pictures. Checked my zipper. Checked that I was still unobserved. Made sure my phone was still in my pocket. And went in.

Halfway through the wires, I felt a sharp tug on the back of my neck.

Craptastic! I'd forgotten to put up the hood. And now it was caught on the wires. I reached back, but I didn't dare untangle it, since I couldn't see behind me. With my luck, I'd definitely touch the electrocution lines. Apparently, electricity was not conveyed through wanna-be camel-colored canvas jackets, though, so I'd gotten lucky with that. I didn't want to push my luck much further. But just as I started to ease through, the hood pulled me off balance, and I had to put my hand down on the wire. With a yelp, I jerked it back and dove through.

This time, I ended up twisted around and flat on my back, hanging halfway upright by the hood of the jacket. Even with the giant yank from my weight hanging on it, it hadn't broken free. I scrambled around, trying in vain to break free. But after five minutes, it was clear I was never going to get loose. I couldn't even rip the jacket. I'd tried.

I pulled out my phone, ready to call the boys, when I realized I didn't have their numbers. Fuming that my mother had handed me a post-it with one of the numbers scrawled on it instead of sending me a text like a normal person, I scrolled through and hit her number. Not her office phone, where her secretary would pretend she didn't know me, and then put me on hold forever like I was a random citizen calling to complain about the homeless guy sleeping on the corner, and then tell me my mother was in a meeting.

No, this called for her personal number, which I was under strict orders not to call unless it was an emergency. Which this clearly was. I could probably lie out here all day before anyone noticed I was gone. From the way they'd both been talking last night, I knew their father didn't like or approve of me and had passed on the gossip about my partying ways and subsequent arrest. The boys would think I ran off to party, and they'd go check all the local bars, leaving me out here to freeze to death and be eaten by coyotes.

"Mom?" I squeaked when she answered on the last ring. I could already picture her pushing her glasses up and pinching the bridge of her nose between her thumb and finger. I could imagine the long-suffering voice she'd use when I asked for Sawyer's number. But I was so relieved that she'd actually answered that I just blurted it out. "Mom, I'm stuck on a cow fence and I can't get off."

Chapter Eleven

AMBER

One Week Earlier

"DO you have any idea how humiliated I am right now?" my mother asked.

"Probably not as humiliated as me," I muttered.

"I had a meeting today, and needless to say, I had to cancel it. If I'd had to cancel my flight this evening…"

"Already?" I asked. "I've barely seen you since you got home."

"You're not a child," Mom snapped. "It's time you started acting your age."

"Can't an adult still want to spend time with her parents?" I asked.

"You're making this very difficult, Amber," Senator Westling said.

"I don't even know what *this* is," I snapped. "Why am I here? What happened?"

"You don't remember?" Senator Westling asked.

"Remember what?"

Mom gave me a long, hard look. "You were arrested last night."

The world swayed unsteadily under my feet. I felt like I was going to get sick.

"What—what happened?" I asked again. "How could I have been arrested?"

"You assaulted Charlie Bontrager," she said, her mouth in a hard line.

"Charlie?" I remembered his Cheshire grin, and the two chicks pleasuring him. A fist of pain punched my hollow heart, but the pain was quickly overtaken by the revelation of what had happened after that. "I threw soup at him," I said, trying not to laugh at the ridiculousness.

"You threw eggs at him," she corrected me. "You and that…friend of yours. I always said she was trouble."

Eggs…a flash of memory of pulling cartons of eggs from Haley's refrigerator, running to the window in our bare feet. "But Mom, you don't understand. He cheated on me. He—"

My mother's palm smacked the table, interrupting me. "I don't care what he did," she yelled.

Senator Westling cleared his throat. "You were *arrested*, Amber. If he presses charges, you'll have a criminal record. This will affect the rest of your life."

"Not to mention mine," Mom said, taking a shaky breath. "I'm up for reelection next year, and my daughter is running around getting arrested? Your lovers' quarrels are your own private affair, Amber. It's time you started behaving like an adult and using a little discretion."

"It's on *Page Six*," Senator Westling said, pushing his tablet towards me.

My stomach lurched, and I had to swallow the urge to puke. I gripped the edge of the table, my throat aching with unshed tears. Moms were supposed to hold their daughters' hands and get them ice cream when they got cheated on. If I opened my mouth to defend myself, I was going to break down in a blubbering, sobbing mess.

"A gossip column," my mother said, sounding as horrified as if I'd made a sex tape. "My daughter cannot be in a gossip column. Do you think Hillary Clinton would be where she is today if Chelsea had been running around getting drunk and being arrested instead of going to an Ivy League school?"

"Bush Senior didn't have any trouble, and his son liked to party," I managed, giving her a hopeful smile.

"They are men," my mother said, slapping the table.

"That's not very fair," I protested, tears burning behind my eyes.

"Grow up, Amber," she snapped. "You should know by now that life's not fair. And it's far past time you straightened up and stopped all this nonsense."

"Okay," I said, swiping at an errant tear. "You're right. I will."

"She's right," Senator Westling said, nosing into our family business like he belonged. Technically, he did, I supposed, but I didn't like it. "It's time you learned a little bit about responsibility and hard work. I never would have learned those lessons myself if I'd grown up here, but I grew up on a ranch in Wyoming. Three of my sons live there now."

"And we've decided you need a break from the business of the city," Mom said, taking the senator's hand. "You've had too much freedom here, going to a private school, doing as you like. We think it's time you learned a little about hard work, discipline, and responsibility in a safe environment."

"Where?"

"With my sons in Wyoming," Senator Westling said.

"You'll be out of the headlines until it's all blown over and is forgotten."

"Babysitting?" I asked incredulously.

"It's not babysitting," my mom said, but she was straight-out lying. I could tell.

Chapter Twelve

AMBER

Now

NOW HERE I WAS, in Wyoming, tied to a cow fence that might electrocute me at any moment. And Mom was pissed at me all over again. But she must not have wanted to actually kill me, because ten minutes later, something that looked like a dusty golf cart rolled onto the grassy path.

Mom had insisted that she would call my stepbrother for me. True to her word, here they were. One of them, anyway. Hoping against hope it was Holden, who probably wouldn't make fun of me the way Sawyer would, I watched the cart bouncing along the road. I wasn't above laughing at myself, once I was out of danger, so I decided I didn't really care who it was at this point, as long as they got me off this damn fence.

The cart rolled to a stop, and a guy I'd never seen before hopped out. My heart nearly stopped beating altogether, and it wasn't because I'd been electrocuted. He had long legs clad in a pair of worn jeans, narrow hips, and broad shoulders inside his flannel shirt. Though he was a bit leaner than the other two, he was just as tall, and even sexier than the two I'd met before. He looked harder, as if he were made of solid steel. His face was weather-worn and tan, with a bit of dark scruff on his cheeks. He looked to be a little older than his brothers, in his late twenties or early thirties. His hair was dark, and so was his scowl.

He strode towards me, his hands balled into fists inside his leather work gloves. His jaw was set, his eyes hard. When he reached me, he towered over me and glared down, making me feel about as big as an ant.

"Is that my jacket?" he asked, his eyes narrowing.

"Maybe?" I asked, giving him my most charming smile, the one that had conned many a bartender into serving me a drink although my fake ID was questionable at best.

"My father called," he said after an awkward moment of silence. "He said you were stuck. Did you break your ankle in those ridiculous boots?"

My mouth fell open, and if I could have pulled myself to my full height, I would have. "For your information, these boots are designed specifically to keep me an extra two inches away from the piles of cow dung in your field," I said.

He snorted, but I was sure a flicker of humor glinted in his eyes.

"And no, I didn't break my ankle, thank you very much. I am quite capable of wearing, and walking in, shoes that are both practical—hence the cow dung barrier—and stylish. But if it makes you happy, I'll take your opinion of my boots into account next time I'm shopping."

"So what's the problem?" he asked. "I thought you were hurt."

"Not hurt," I said, tugging at the edge of the hood to show him. "Stuck."

He bent over me, and I caught a whiff of pine needles and something as wild as the west wind. My heart tripped in my chest, and I had to resist the urge to close my eyes and inhale him like the chilled Wyoming breeze across the grass.

He pinched the fabric of my hood, and with one tug, I was free. I jumped to my feet and dusted myself off.

"Sorry about the jacket," I said. "I was just going to wear it to step outside, but then I wanted to see what those yellow trees were, and…"

He glared at me.

"And I got stuck," I finished, gulping down a sudden bout of nerves.

"Christ, this really is a babysitting job," he muttered. "You couldn't pull a quarter-inch barb out of a piece of canvas?"

"I could, but I didn't want to get electrocuted."

"What are you on about now?"

"Holden told me to be careful of the electric fences."

Cursing under his breath, he shook his head. I wracked my brain for his name, but I couldn't come up with it, so I thrust my hand out. "I'm Amber," I said. "Thank you for coming out here to get me. If I could have pulled the hood off the fence without touching the wire, I would have. I just couldn't see it from that angle."

"Barbed wire isn't electrified," he said flatly.

"What?"

He wrapped a hand around the top strand of wire and leaned on it, crossing his feet and looking me up and down. Suddenly, I felt not just small, but very naked and very stupid.

Suddenly, Chatty Amber bubbled up. "I had no idea,"

I said. "And although you might think I'm a total dumbass for getting stuck on your fence when it was apparently an easy fix, I have never actually seen a barbed wire fence, or any kind of wire fence, for that matter. You don't have to babysit me, but you might have to forgive my ignorance of farm life. For what it's worth, if I ever invited you to New York City, I wouldn't expect you to know how to get a taxi or have the subway map memorized."

When I saw Waylon's taken-aback expression, I slapped a hand over my mouth, stopping a further flood of words. To my surprise, Waylon nodded, pressing his lips together. "You're right," he said. "I'm being a complete ass."

"Well, maybe not a complete ass," I said. "But at least a half ass."

Waylon smiled, and his whole face changed, the coldness melting away like the first warm day after a long winter. "Can't have that," he said. "I'm of the 'go big or go home' frame of mind."

"I can't go home for three months," I said. "So I guess I better go big."

Waylon shook his head and hopped up into the cart, grabbing the top to swing himself up and in. "Hop on up and hold on tight," he said, patting the dusty leather seat beside him. "You're in for a wild ride, Princess."

"I think I can handle it," I said with a smirk, hopping up beside him.

"We'll see," he said, swinging the cart around in a tight circle. "If you're planning to stick, you might as well learn the lay of the land."

"Really?" I asked, perking up. "Can we go see those yellow trees?"

He started towards the trees, away from the house,

along the narrow trail I'd walked down before I got distracted by the cows.

"Thanks," I said after a minute of bouncing up and down in the seat. It was hard not to notice the rocking motion of it when I was so close to such a hot man.

A hot man who's your brother, I reminded myself.

"It must be hard to come out here by yourself," he said after a minute of listening to nothing but the hum of the motor. "Not knowing anyone or anything."

"I don't know what you're talking about," I said. "I know everything."

"I know better than to disagree when a woman says that," he said as the cart crested a little swell in the land and started down the other side. Ahead, I could see the line of yellow trees. They were tall and thin, with white bark and bright yellow leaves that cheered up the whole place.

"Are those birch trees?" I asked.

"Aspen."

"Okay, maybe I don't know *everything*," I admitted. "But I'm sure you can fix that."

He gave me a funny look, opened his mouth, then closed it and stared straight ahead, his fingers gripping the steering wheel and his brows drawing together.

"So, um, is this still your ranch?" I asked, twisting around to look back at the house. It was probably five blocks away, but there was not a single thing standing between it and where we were. Unless cows counted.

"Uh-huh," Waylon said. The cart passed from the field into a stand of trees, and I leaned back to look up at the yellow leaves contrasting against the clear blue sky, which had never looked so big or bright back home. Just then, the cart did a nose-dive.

I screamed and grabbed onto the dash with one hand and Waylon with the other. We bounced down into a ditch at least as deep as the cart. The tires ground and skidded on sand and round, smooth stones. My butt bounced at least a foot into the air despite my grip on the dash and my stepbrother.

Waylon shot me a grin, shifted gears, and hit the gas pedal. The cart lurched forward, lumbering up the other side, tilting so far we were nearly flat on our backs. When it bounced onto flat ground again, I tried to catch my breath.

"Some grip you got there," Waylon said.

I looked down, only then realizing I was still clutching his thigh. It was solid muscle under my hand, hot and hard inside my tight grip. And I didn't want to let go.

I jerked my hand back and smoothed my hair, which had flown all over the place in the turmoil. "You could have given me some warning."

"I told you to hang on tight," he said. "The creek bed is about halfway across the ranch. It only flows part of the year. We got access to the river a little further on, and five ponds on the property, too."

"My God, you must own as much land as the island of Manhattan," I said, marveling at the new expanse of land.

"For now," Waylon muttered, shifting gears.

"What do you mean?"

"Nothing," he said, shaking his head. "We're almost to the river. You gonna be mad if I get you a little wet there, Princess?"

Chapter Thirteen

AMBER

Now

BY THE TIME we got back to the house after riding around the entire property on the cart, which Waylon called a side-by-side, the tinge of embarrassment over getting stuck on the fence had disappeared. But when we got back to the house, Waylon switched off the motor and turned to me.

"If you don't mind, can you…not tell the others?" I said. "I don't want all three of you thinking I'm a ditzy dumbass."

"I don't think that," Waylon said in a low voice, his eyes locked on mine. A jolt went through me, and my heart trembled. I found my gaze dropping to his smooth, angular mouth. His eyes explored my face, too, but he pulled away and turned to face the big house in front of us. He lifted his hat, ran a hand over his short black hair, and shook his head. "I won't say anything if you don't want me to," he said. "But I don't think you give my brothers enough credit."

"Just give it a few days, until I've actually done something right. Then I'll tell them."

He nodded. "Good. We share everything. I don't like keeping secrets."

"Thank you." And then, because I was feeling both grateful and daring, and a little crazy from the wild ride, I leaned over and gave him a quick kiss on his scratchy cheek before slipping out of the vehicle and darting towards the house. I had worked up the courage to do that, but I didn't dare look back until I was inside the house.

I ran up to my room to call Haley. "Oh my gosh, Amber," she said. "How are you? I've been so bored without you. How's Wyoming? Are the boys good, or are they little snots?"

"Um. One of them might be a big snot, but I think I'm growing on him," I said, stepping up to my window and pulling aside the thin white curtain.

Waylon was sitting in the side-by-side, staring off, his fingertips resting against his cheek where I'd kissed him. A shivery feeling went through me again.

"Explain," Haley demanded. I quickly filled her in on the details of the night before and that morning, including the incident of getting stuck on the fence. Since I knew she wouldn't judge me, I didn't hold back, and we were soon laughing our asses off.

When we finally recovered, Haley said, "At least one of us isn't bored. I'd rather be sent off to a rehab ranch than stuck here on house arrest."

"You'll be fine," I promised. "It's just three months. What's the worst that could happen?"

"Nothing," she agreed. "I'm not allowed to leave the house on my own. So nothing will happen here. And you're in the middle of nowhere, so it's not like you can get in trouble even if you tried."

I thought of Sawyer's blue eyes scoping me out. "Exactly," I said.

"And if those boys act in any way but brotherly, I will break my house arrest and fly out there to personally kick their asses," Haley added.

"I might not mind," I said, remembering the hardness of Waylon's thigh under my hand.

"Amber," Haley shrieked. "You're so bad!"

"You're one to talk."

She sighed. "I know. I'm sorry I got you into this mess."

"No way," I said. "It was my boyfriend who called the cops when we egged him. What a complete wuss."

"I have to tell you something," Haley said. "I should have told you sooner."

My stomach flipped, and I gripped the phone tighter. "What? Did he call?"

"No," she said. "Amber, it really was my fault. It was my idea to egg him. I'm so sorry. You might have been too drunk to know better, but I wasn't."

"Shut up," I said. "I threw the eggs, too, didn't I? I don't think you made me do anything."

"Yeah, but I got you arrested."

"No more than I got you arrested. It was my boyfriend we were egging. He's the one who got us both arrested."

"Yeah," she said. "But I'm still sorry."

"Don't even mention it," I said. "You'd have done the same for me."

And I knew she would. There was a reason we'd never been apart more than a few weeks. I could trust Haley with anything, could trust her to the ends of the earth. She'd never judge me for anything, from being arrested to getting caught on a barbed wire fence to thinking my own stepbrothers were total hotties.

Chapter Fourteen

HOLDEN

AFTER LUNCH, I realized I hadn't seen Amber since that morning, when I'd peeked in her door and saw her slumbering on the pillows in the bed that used to be Waylon's.

I shook my head, not wanting to think of Maria. It was hard not to, though, with a woman in the house again. It was hard not to let the ghosts come back and remind us of what happened last time. It was hard not to watch Amber for comparisons.

"Anyone seen our sister?" I asked, standing from the table and picking up the plate I'd made for her.

Waylon flinched. "She's not our sister."

"Stepsister," I said. It was true, she wasn't one of us. She hadn't grown up with us, didn't know our secrets and our pasts the way we knew each other's.

"She went out back," Sawyer said.

"To the cabins?" I asked, my belly taking a dive. A selfish instinct to protect the cabins, to keep everyone away from them, made my fists clench around the edges of the plate I was holding.

"They're on the property," Sawyer said, as if it didn't

matter. But I knew it mattered to all of us. Letting her see the cabins was really letting her into our lives, into ourselves. It was like if we'd read her diaries.

"Mine's locked," Waylon said, stuffing his mouth with the last bite of his sandwich.

"Really?" I asked. When he didn't answer, I pressed. "Why?"

He shrugged. "Nobody uses it. No reason for anyone to wander in, thinking it's a garden shed."

The thought almost made me laugh, but I frowned instead. I didn't push it, though there was no way in hell anyone could mistake the cabins for garden sheds. They looked like exactly what they were—small log cabins. But if Waylon wanted to keep his locked up, it was none of my business.

I headed out back with the plate for Amber.

Amber.

I whispered her name to myself as I headed for the first cabin, the door of which stood open. Her name was so right, like a gem on my tongue. When I said it, warmth filled my belly like I'd just drunk a mug of warm apple cider spiked with whiskey on a long, bitter winter's night.

As I climbed the steps, I was aware of how heavy my footsteps were, how the stairs creaked under my weight and the cabin shivered as I crossed the porch.

"What are these?" Amber called from inside.

"They're…cabins," I said, stepping inside. The room was dim without lights on, but I could see Amber standing in the center of the open floor, looking up at the beams above.

"I can see that," she said. "Who lives here?"

I shrugged. "No one. Want a sandwich?"

She looked at me as if just realizing I was there. It took a second for her blue eyes to clear. I studied her face, trying to figure what she might be thinking. Her sexy, full lips were bare of lipstick today, which made her look younger than she had the night before. I reminded myself she was my little sister before I could linger on her long, lean figure too long.

"You made me lunch?" she asked, then bounded over, her long hair bouncing behind her. "Thank you. That's so sweet."

I cleared my throat and looked around the place. It hadn't been touched in years, not since we'd moved into the big house and decided nothing would ever come between us again.

"So what's up with them?" Amber asked through a mouthful of sandwich, wiping the corner of her lips on her wrist.

It took me a second to tear my eyes away from her lips. They seemed to have a hypnotic effect on me. "They're our houses," he said. "Our grandfather built them, hoping to keep all his sons in the business. He's the one who started Coyote Ranch."

"Wow," she said, nodding. "So you have these five houses, plus the big lodge. You should rent them out."

I choked on that thought. "I don't think Waylon would go for that."

"I can see that," she said, her eyes narrowing as she studied the stairs to the loft. "He seems kind of private."

"He's a good man," I said. "You'll see once you get to know him."

"I know," Amber said, which surprised me. Had Waylon already warmed up to her? That was unheard of. Waylon was always the one who found something missing in the women we brought home. Since Maria, he'd had nothing but criticism for any woman we showed interest in.

I was going about this all wrong, though. Amber wasn't

a woman we'd brought home. She wasn't a potential partner for any of us, or even a potential fuck. She was our stepsister. The daughter of the woman Dad had married before anyone in his family had even met her. Just because she slept down the hall from us didn't make her available.

Amber went to the stairs and sat down, patting the step beside her. After a second, I approached, but I tried to keep my distance as I sat down beside her. I was an oaf taking up most of the width of the stairs next to her trim shoulders, though, and our shoulders brushed against each other.

"Tell me something," she said.

"Uh huh," I said, wary of her questions.

"Sawyer told me none of you are married. How is that possible? Just look at you." She made a choking sound and rushed ahead, her words coming so fast it made my head spin. "I mean, not saying anything, but seriously. You're all good-looking guys. In the old days, people would have thought you were gay. But now that it's legal, even that wouldn't stop you from getting married. So what's the deal?"

She stopped talking and nibbled at her sandwich, looking at me expectantly. I started turning over answers in my mind, but before a minute was up, she must have decided I wasn't going to answer. New York must move at warp speed. Even her talking was fast.

"And look at this place. You could have five little families living in these cabins, have your kids all growing up together. Plus, you have that huge lodge. You're a catch. All of you are. Are there just not enough women up here in the wilderness or what? Because otherwise, I don't get it."

I shrugged, not sure how to answer that question without making her think I was all kinds of sick in the head. "We're a team," I said at last. "Like any good team, we all have our individual roles, but as a whole, we have one goal. What's best for one of us is best for all of us."

"And…women aren't good for you?"

"Not so far," I said. "Women who see us as a catch are just after what we have. And right now we're barely holding onto the ranch."

Amber nodded, chewing slowly. "I get it. You don't need the distraction. And you don't want someone who's only after your money."

"Exactly," I said, relieved to let her do the talking.

"It's hard to find someone who's interested in you for who you really are," she said. "I thought out here, people might be more…transparent, I guess. All the people at my school were so driven, which is good, but it's also like, they only wanted you for what you could do for them. It's almost like in the old days, when people only married for political gain. Except at school, people were *dating* for those reasons."

"Sounds like a lot of drama."

"It was," she said with a sigh. "I'm so glad to be done with it. My parents literally chose who I could date in high school."

I pulled back to look at her. "Why'd you let them?"

"I don't know," she said with a shrug, her blonde hair cascading over her shoulder. "I never really liked anyone I couldn't date, so it didn't matter that much to me. If I'd been in love with someone else, it would have been different. But I wasn't, and I guess I wanted to make my parents happy. They may be jerks sometimes, but they're still my parents."

I had a strange urge to pull her into my arms, to brush that hair back from her face and tell her we'd never do something like that to her, that she was safe now.

"A lot of people's parents did that at my school," she

said. "That's one of the reasons I wanted to leave the country with my best friend. Just to get away from it for a while, get to really be ourselves, away from gossip blogs and news hounds."

"That sounds like a good thing," I said. "Doesn't your mom want that, too? That's why she sent you out here."

"She sent me out here as punishment," Amber said. "And to get me out of the spotlight. I think she's afraid I'd make some kind of international scandal if I went overseas. But she's already probably plotting who I need to be friends with at college. As soon as I start school again, my parents are going to want to know who's going to the same university as me, and how I can arrange my schedule to get in classes with the important ones. It's so orchestrated."

"I can't imagine living that way," I said, shaking my head. "Out here, we do as we want. We have an understanding with other ranchers and folks around here. Our rules are sometimes a little different from the law. But we make it work."

She grinned sideways at me. "It's like you're still living in the wild west."

"It can get a little wild," I admitted.

Amber sighed and set her plate between her feet. "I wish I had that much freedom. My two boyfriends in high school were both chosen by my parents. They each got to pick one. It was a source of conflict, of course, like everything else. My mom didn't like the guy my dad picked, when we broke up, she blamed it all on him. And then the guy she picked…well, let's just say I'd rather not talk about him. Just once, I'd like to pick my own relationship with someone my parents don't choose for me. Someone with a less than stellar approval rating, or someone completely politically incorrect. You know what I mean?"

Did I ever.

Chapter Fifteen

AMBER

THAT EVENING, as I was hanging out in my room, the unmistakable scent of frying onions wafted up from the kitchen. Curiosity got the better of me, and I headed downstairs. When I stepped into the kitchen, I found Sawyer standing at the stove, stirring the onions in a black cast iron skillet.

"You cook?" I asked.

He turned, the wooden spoon still held in one hand, and gave me that knee-melting smile. "Sure do," he said. "I hope you're hungry."

"So hungry," I said, unable to keep my eyes from roaming over his arms. God, it was impossible to resist all these gorgeous guys in one place.

"Good," Sawyer said, turning back to the counter. "We've got plenty."

"There must be something on the wind up here," I said, joining Sawyer at the counter, where he was chopping peppers on a wooden cutting board. "I've never been so hungry in my life."

Or so horny.

"Is that right?" Sawyer asked, cocking an eyebrow as if he knew exactly what I was thinking.

"Want some help?" I scooted a little closer, until the heat of his skin zipped up my arm. I closed my eyes and tried not to melt.

"You cook?" Sawyer asked, pulling back to look at me.

"I actually love cooking," I admitted.

"Really?" Sawyer asked, sounding impressed.

"But don't even think about asking me to be your cook for the next three months. Or wash your underwear, or any of those other old-fashioned notions you men probably have about where women belong."

"Us men?" he asked, shaking his head. "Maybe you're the one with the old-fashioned notions."

"You're burning the onions." I plucked the wooden spoon from the counter and stirred the onions while Sawyer dumped in a handful of diced peppers.

"I thought you didn't want to be our cook," Sawyer teased, nudging me with his elbow.

"That doesn't mean I won't help out," I said. "I'm living here, too, now. I don't expect you to wait on me."

"Okay, Princess."

"Quit that," I said, elbowing him back.

"Yes, Your Highness."

I laughed as I stirred the frying vegetables. "So do the others cook? Or just you?"

"We share cooking duties," he said. "But I do most of it. I like to cook. It's relaxing."

"I just like making things," I said. "Trying new recipes, seeing how flavors work together. Sometimes the most unexpected combination of ingredients turns out to be the perfect one."

I reached for the garlic he'd minced on the board at the same moment he did. Our fingers touched, and we both paused. Neither of us pulled away. Slowly, Sawyer hand slid over mine, his calloused fingers tightening over my soft ones. I caught him watching my lips, and heat spread up my neck. That was not a brotherly look on his face.

My heart hammered so hard in my chest I thought I'd explode. I wet my lips and leaned in a fraction of an inch, just enough for him to see it. An invitation.

Just then, Sawyer's phone rang. He cleared his throat and pulled his hand away, turning from me and scooping up the garlic with the edge of the knife. He dumped it into the pan and stirred it, moving so his back was to me.

What the hell had just happened? He shouldn't have been looking at me that way. And I shouldn't have liked it. But he was, and I did.

"Our mom taught us to cook," Sawyer said, pulling his phone out just long enough to silence the ringer before dropping it back into his pocket. "She can make damn near anything. What about you?"

I shook my head to clear it. I must have imagined that lustful look in his hooded eyes.

"Um, no, not so much," I said. Sawyer handed me the spoon and skirted around me, like he was afraid of accidentally touching me. He went to the fridge, got out some meat, and started slicing it. Meanwhile, I went straight into verbal-vomit mode.

"Well, actually, I don't really know if my mom can cook, but I've never seen her try," I said. "She's so busy, she'd probably forget she put on toast until the house burnt down. When I was growing up, we had a nanny who cooked. She's the one who taught me. I'd come home from school every day and do my homework at the kitchen table while she cooked. It always smelled so good, and eventually, I wanted to know how to make food like that. So it became something we did together. I loved spending time with her, since my parents were always gone. There's something really satisfying about feeding people, about being able to satisfy them."

"I couldn't agree more," Sawyer said. There was an underlying current of tension still sizzling in the air around us. And though his words were slightly teasing, laced with some added meaning, the reminder of that moment that shouldn't have happened remained.

"It's nice to take something you made and share it with another person," I said. "It's like sharing a part of yourself."

"Especially if you make it together," Sawyer said.

"Of course," I said. "Everything's better together."

Chapter Sixteen

AMBER

A WEEK LATER, I'd explored everything there was to see, except four of the cabins out back. While the boys were out working, I stood on the back porch, holding a mug of tea between my hands to warm them, and studied them. They stood in a row, set at a forty-five-degree angle from the house. The first one was just across an expanse of lawn, but the furthest one, where the Grimeses lived, was quite a way off.

Though I went into one the first day, I hadn't been inside the others. It felt weird to go in somewhere that Mrs. Grimes said was private to them, even if they didn't tell me not to. Still, I could see the potential. I'd been turning it over in my head since Holden told me they were barely holding onto the ranch. Now it was time to put it out there.

I turned and headed back inside to make dinner. True to his word, Sawyer didn't try to saddle me with the domestic tasks, but I'd asked to be put on the cooking rotation. I wasn't there for a free ride.

Once the table was set with dishes and a vase of dried wildflowers in the center, I went out back and ring the big dinner bell. Every time I rang it, I felt like Lady Liberty ringing the Liberty Bell. I keep that little tidbit to myself as I stood tall and regal and let the gong ring out across the yard. And yes, I was aware that Lady Liberty didn't actually ring the bell.

A few minutes later, when everyone was seated at the table and eating, I took a deep breath. "Guess what I did today?"

"Got caught on a barbed wire fence?" Waylon asked, cocking an eyebrow at me.

I gave him a murderous glare. "No," I said slowly. "I got to thinking about the cabins."

"You want one, right?" Waylon said, setting down his fork and bracing the heels of his hands on the table edge. "The fourth one. We each have one, and the Grimes are living in the fifth. And since our father married your mother, you think you get a piece of the ranch."

"What? No." I couldn't help but feel the sting of his words. I couldn't believe he thought that about me, that I was after their money.

"What about the cabins, Amber?" Holden asked, giving me an encouraging smile.

"Well, you had mentioned maybe you were in a little financial trouble," I said. "And I thought that since you have four houses out there…I mean, they're small, but they're cute cabins. Maybe you could set up some kind of bed-and-breakfast type thing. Or at least rent them out on Air B&B. You don't have to do anything for that. It rents out as-is, and you can do it during the tourist season, when people come up to ski, and also in the off season, when they come up to go to the Tetons."

"No," Waylon said, not looking up from his chicken parmesan.

"Why not?" I asked. "I get that you don't want

strangers hanging around, but come on. You already have Mrs. Grimes, and she's nosy as hell. And if you need money…"

"No," he said again, raising his eyes this time. To my surprise, they were flashing with anger.

"Hear her out, Waylon," Sawyer said.

"Okay then," I said. "If you're so protective of them, why don't you move out there and rent out this place? It's huge. You could get a whole bunch of people to rent the lodge at once, and you'd have your privacy out back."

"You don't know anything about this place," Waylon said. "You can't just come in here for a week and start making changes. That's not how this works."

"Then enlighten me," I said. "How does it work? I'm just supposed to sit up in my room and stay out of the way for three months? And then when I leave, you can forget I was ever here at all?"

Waylon's stormy grey eyes were hard as slate. "Exactly."

"That might work if we weren't related," I said, shooting him a triumphant smile. Maybe I was gloating a little. But he couldn't get rid of me that easily. If I was stuck with him for the rest of my life, then he was stuck with me. We were all in the same shitty situation together—thrown together by our parents, who couldn't even be bothered to tell us before they got married.

"We're not related," Waylon said, his brows lowered in a fierce glare. "We're blood brothers. You're just a busybody like Mrs. Grimes, living on our property and poking into our business. I suggest you stay out of it."

"I suggest you get used to it," I said. "Because I'm here to stay. If not on your ranch, at least in your life. And don't count on me making it easy for you to forget it."

To my horror, my throat constricted painfully, and my

eyes ached with unshed tears. They threatened to burst forth at any minute, but I wasn't going to let this jerk make me cry. At least not where he could see it.

"Enjoy your dinner," I said. I stalked out of the kitchen, grabbed my jacket from the rack, and headed out into the bitter cold twilight. I hoped they felt guilty for sitting around the table eating the dinner I had cooked for them. Part of me was furious at Waylon, but a little part of me knew he was right. Here, just like at home, I was dispensable.

Sure, they might enjoy the chicken I'd made for dinner, but if I hadn't been there, someone else would have cooked. They wouldn't miss me. I hadn't made a notable contribution, and Waylon had let me know it. He'd told me exactly where I stood. I was a nuisance—a forgettable nuisance.

I thought of all the times my parents had made me feel exactly like that. Classes they'd signed me up for, only to shove me off on the nanny. It was her job to take me to ballet, gymnastics, piano, painting, tennis, horseback riding… When I had a recital or a match, they'd forget as often as not. And when they did come, they'd spend most of their time ducking out to take phone calls. They'd let me know in not-so-subtle ways that I was a pain in their very busy asses.

Ducking my head, I hurried past the barn and stables, along one of the wide paths the guys drove around the ranch on. This one was wider, the tracks worn down to dirt with just a bit of dried up brown grass in the middle. A cow mooed at me from across the field.

Of course, as I'd grown older, I'd found ways to make myself less forgettable, though I was still a nuisance to my parents. Getting in trouble was at least memorable—not to mention fun. And I'd found a partner in crime in Haley, someone who never made me feel unimportant or stupid, boring or annoying.

I smiled to myself as I walked. I still owed her a good cow picture. It was a little dark, but the cows were crowded around a feeder up ahead, chowing down on some new hay bales the guys had put out that evening.

I stopped and felt for my phone, relieved to find it in my back pocket. This was the perfect opportunity to get close enough to snap a picture, while the cows were distracted by their food. Hurrying along the road, I kept my eye on them until I drew closer, then I pushed apart the strands of barbed wire and squeezed through. It was easier now that I knew they weren't going to electrocute me.

Stealthy as a coyote, I crept towards the cows. I wasn't actually sure coyotes were stealthy, but I figured they must be to take down one of these beasts. As I drew closer, I could see the sheer size of them. Their jaws worked, and I could hear their grinding teeth from twenty feet away. Each one must have been a ton of solid muscle. My heart beat faster as I slunk even closer, picking my way around stinky piles of manure.

"Here, Bessie," I coaxed in a voice barely above a whisper.

A cow lifted its head and stared at me. Holy crapoli! I hadn't actually known one of them was named Bessie.

She stared at me a long moment, raised her tail, and shot a stream of hot, steaming urine onto the ground. I tried not to recoil in disgust. Bessie plodded into the herd, her big hips bumping the other cows, who shuffled and moved restlessly around the bale of hay. I circled a huge black tub of water that sat nearby, a tank suspended above it. And then I was there, so close I could see the breath puffing from the cows into the cold night. I could smell them, too—the warm animal smell of them, the smell of their waste, of rotting grass and dry hay and a tinge of mold.

"Here, Bessie," I said, hoping the cow would turn around. It was too dark to get a good picture unless I used the flash, and I wanted to make sure she was looking when I took my one shot. I figured she'd freak out and run when the flash went off, maybe cause a stampede. That would give Waylon something to remember.

"Here, Bessie Bessie Bessie," I coaxed. One of the other cows swung its giant head towards me. Its eyes disappeared into its solid black fur, so it looked like some kind of weird, blind mutant. I could only hope it would look like a cow and not a freaky sasquatch in the photo. Holding firmly to that hope, I snapped the picture.

The dumb old thing didn't even move when the flash went off. I took the opportunity to check out the photo. But when I looked up, the beast was advancing on me at a trot.

I screamed and turned to run, but I ran smack into the edge of the water trough. Panicked, I bounced back from the plastic wall of the thing, only to see the black monster bearing down. It was only a few steps away.

"Go away," I said, holding out a hand, as if I could stop it.

The giant sort of skipped its legs sideways, like it was having the time of its life teasing me as it prepared to skewer me. It would probably run around the ranch carrying my head on its horn like a trophy in some barbaric cow ritual.

And then I remembered seeing a couple minutes of a rodeo—or maybe it was a bullfight—in a movie. The bull skipped around just like that.

Oh shit. I'd forgotten about the bull. What if it couldn't see in the darkness that my jacket was actually burgundy and not red?

It skipped towards me again. I turned and bolted. I expected a horn to fatally gouge me at any moment. That would give stupid Waylon something to remember. I'd be dead, so I wouldn't be here to enjoy it, but it would serve his smug ass right.

Instead of being hit from behind, I was hit across the thighs. More accurately, I hit something. Arms pinwheeling, I gave a blood curdling scream before I promptly sprawled headlong into the water trough.

Chapter Seventeen

AMBER

THE WATER WAS SO cold I couldn't move for a second. I just lay there like a frozen corpse at the bottom of an icy sea. But after a second, I thought of the bottom-feeders that would come to devour me, and I scrambled to get up. My head broke the surface, and if anything, the air felt even colder than the breath-stealing water. I flailed my arms, gasping in a breath. To my horror, the bull was hovering over the trough, waiting to take me down.

Double shit. It was either die a slow death by freezing in the trough, or get skewered by a longhorn.

I figured the second sounded better—more glorious, like a cowgirl in the old west. But the choice was harder than it sounded, because I really wasn't keen on dying tonight. I huddled against the tank of water, away from the horns of the bulls. In fact, there were two now—the black one, with the short horns, and a longhorn. So if one of them didn't get me, the other would.

I reached for my phone, but my heart sank as I patted my pockets. I'd been taking a picture when the bull noticed me, so I'd had it in my hand. Which meant it had already met its end by one of the two means I was now facing. It was either out there being trampled by vicious bulls or lying at the bottom of the trough in a watery grave.

No phone. No weapons. No escape.

I didn't even have anything to throw to distract the bulls. My hands were so cold I didn't know if I could have closed them around a rock or something if I had it, let alone punch in numbers on a phone. It took several attempts just to pull my sodden jacket closed around me. Everything on my body ached with cold from my toes to my scalp, and I had skipped straight past shivering to quaking.

I had one hope left.

I started to scream.

It turned out the cows didn't like screaming very much, and they actually backed off a few feet. But I had no doubt the second I stepped out, they'd barrel down on me, banshee shrieking or not. I could only hope the boys could hear me from the house and didn't think it was just the wind.

And then my heart sank. They were running the tractors for some reason. They'd never hear me over the loud engines. I could see lights far off and here the engines on the path that I'd walked the first day, when I'd gotten stuck in the fence. Maybe they were looking for me. Surely, they didn't think I was dumb enough to get stuck on the fence twice!

When I looked around me, I swallowed that little seed of pride. Hell, maybe I'd rather die than have them come to my rescue now, anyway. I'd never live this one down.

But when I faced the possibility that I might actually die, I knew that wasn't the case. I started screaming at the top of my lungs again.

After a few minutes, lights washed over the tank. They

were going to miss me! I was huddled too close to the tank. So I jumped towards the edge, spooking the cows back another few feet, and waved wildly for an entire minute, which wasn't easy with my limbs seizing up from cold.

At last, the lights stopped moving on the path. I could hear the tractor idling, but I couldn't tell if anyone had gotten out. A second later, though, Waylon came hurtling over the fence.

He waved his arm in a shooing motion at the cows and yelled, "Hya! Hya!" And they all scooted back.

He ran over to the water trough, grabbed me around the waist, and lifted me out. "What the hell are you doing in there?" he demanded, peeling off my jacket. "It's twenty degrees out here."

"I f-f-fell in," I chattered through my teeth, trying to fight his hands. Was he seriously trying to undress me right now?

He brushed my hands away like they were nothing more than annoying flies, grabbed the bottom of my shirt, and wrenched it over my head. "Why didn't you get out and run back to the house?" he barked. "Were you stuck?"

"N-no."

"You're going to get hypothermia."

"Exactly," I managed, falling back against the trough as he unzipped my pants. "So why are you taking off my clothes?"

"Stop fighting me," he said. "Wet clothes suck the heat right out of you. You got only a couple minutes to get out of them before hypothermia sets in."

It was probably too late for that, but I didn't seem able to form the words. Waylon had peeled my jeans down, and my underwear had gone with them, and he didn't say a word about it or try to pull them up like a decent person. He just peeled them off over my feet, along with my shoes.

Then he threw me over his shoulder like a sack of oats for his horses, with my bare ass sticking straight out for all the world to see, and ran for the fence. Even with me on his shoulder, her hopped it with seeming ease. Then he hopped up into the tractor and pulled me in with him.

I ended up on his lap. Naked. But it was not exactly the way it had been in the fantasies I'd been having since arriving at Coyote Ranch. I was too cold to be embarrassed, though, and luckily, the tractor wasn't one of those old ones with a metal seat and an exposed top. No, this was a huge one with lights, and closed-in cab with heat. Waylon turned the heat on full blast and looked at me. He swallowed so hard I could see his Adam's apple move up and down.

Then he scooted me off his lap, peeled off his own jacket, and put it around me.

I pulled it tight. "Th-thank you," I chattered.

Waylon looked at me another moment, then lifted up his hips, unbuttoned the shoulders of his tan, canvas coveralls, and began to undress.

It wasn't the most romantic moment I could imagine for getting laid. But then, I was going to have to get properly laid eventually, and I'd never had a romantic moment. My only long-term boyfriend had been a frigid, misogynist pig who wanted to lock me in a chastity belt while he galivanted around Manhattan letting redheads ride his face for fun.

But when Waylon slipped out of his coveralls, he was wearing a pair of thin black pants under them. He leaned over and pooled the coveralls at my feet, slowly working them up over my legs. They were heavily lined, and warm inside from his body heat, but I didn't think I'd ever get warm again. Waylon sat back, cranked the tractor into gear, and we hurtled along the bumpy path.

Finally, we reached a spot where we could turn around, and Waylon turned the tractor back towards the house. I was starting to regain feeling in my limbs at last, but Waylon was still shooting me concerned looks every two seconds.

When I heard him curse under his breath, I looked up to see a flashlight beam in the path. Waylon honked the horn, then cursed louder, braking fast enough to make me almost slide off the seat.

"Yoo-hoo," tootled a familiar voice.

Craptastic. Mrs. Grimes had stopped us for a chat.

Waylon rolled down his window and tried to wave her away.

"I heard a commotion, and I just had to come make sure everything was okay," she said, coming around the side of the tractor. As soon as she was out of the path, Waylon shifted gears, and the tractor rolled forward.

"Now hold up," Mrs. Grimes called, but Waylon paid her no mind. He drove straight up to the doors of the lodge, jumped out, and ran around to my side of the tractor. Opening the door, he scooped me into his arms and ran inside.

"What happened?" Sawyer asked, rushing to my side.

"I fell in the cow water," I managed.

Waylon carried me to the fireplace and laid me on the bearskin rug. This was probably not the appropriate time to think about how sexy it was to have this rugged cowboy laying me down in front of the fire like he was about to ravish me. So I blamed the hypothermia for that thought. I was, after all, bedraggled as a wet rat, half-frozen, and wearing a pair of men's coveralls. But damn if they weren't the warmest thing I'd ever worn in my entire life. I was totally putting a pair on my Christmas list, and I was going to wear them all over Manhattan until it became a major fashion trend. Or at least until my mom's strategists told her to make me stop.

Waylon took my hand and started rubbing up and down my arm. "We need to get her warmed up," he said.

I could think of something he could rub that would get me warm a lot faster, but then, I probably wasn't supposed to think something like that about my stepbrothers, let alone say it aloud.

Sawyer knelt at my other side and, before I could warn him, unzipped Waylon's jacket. His eyes widened, and his mouth fell open and then closed without a word coming out. "Oh," he said, his voice slightly choked.

Just then, the door flew open, and Holden stepped inside. He pulled up short, the heels of his cowboy boots probably leaving skid marks on the hardwood. His eyes just about popped out of his head.

Not gonna lie, I was not entirely comfortable with my nipples on full display for my three sexy stepbrothers to stand around ogling.

But I was not entirely uncomfortable, either.

A sense of power swelled inside me as Holden rushed to the couch to gather blankets, and Waylon rubbed feeling into my arms, and Sawyer sat there staring at my nips like they were made of rubies. I could have sat up, or pushed them away, or grabbed my jacket closed. But I didn't want to. For once, just this once, I wanted to enjoy being the center of attention.

For once, I wasn't doing something bad just to get that attention. I wasn't drinking or puking or threatening to hook up with someone from the libertarian party. I wasn't getting my picture taken by a photographer who might extort my mother to get it hidden. I wasn't putting my leg behind my head at a bar while wearing a skirt.

For once, it was all about me. I wasn't doing it for

anyone else. It was just me, and just them, and maybe I deserved to have someone pay attention to me for some reason other than what I'd done wrong.

So for just for a minute, I let myself feel the warmth spreading through my body as Waylon's strong, capable fingers massaged my muscles. I let myself enjoy the concern in Holden's eyes when he dropped to his knees and spread a thick blanket over me. I let myself soak up Sawyer's admiration as he slowly eased off the jacket and dropped it on the floor beside him.

His hand closed around mine at the same moment Waylon found my other hand again after dropping it to help remove his jacket from around me. This time, his fingers moved slowly up my bare arm, sending fire racing through my veins. His grip was firm, his thumb pressing deep against my muscle as he slowly massaged the feeling into my right arm. Sawyer held my left hand, his strokes quick and agitated as he tried to get my blood flowing faster. Holden knelt above me, gently rubbing my hair with a towel.

The sensation warmed a lot more than my arms. As my cold shudders subsided, tingles took over, racing across my body and down my belly, building pressure between my legs.

I couldn't decide where to look, at Sawyer's burning, intense eyes or Waylon's stormy, dark ones. So I looked instead at Holden, whose earnest expression of concern almost broke my heart. His fingers slowed when our eyes met, then slipped from the towel into my hair. Electricity sizzled through my body, and before I could stop myself, a moan escaped my lips.

And then the front door flew open and a blast of icy wind swept across the room, along with the scrutinizing gaze of one Mrs. Grimes, elderly neighbor and caretaker.

Chapter Eighteen

AMBER

I MIGHT HAVE LAUGHED at the horrified, scandalized expression on Mrs. Grimes's face, but since I was currently half naked and in a state of pure bliss, I decided to shut my mouth this once and let the guys do the talking.

"Well, I never," Mrs. Grimes cried. "I heard quite a commotion earlier, but this!"

"Mrs. Grimes," Waylon said, withdrawing his hand from under my blanket and rising halfway.

"What on earth is going on in this house?" she demanded, fisting her hands on her hips. "I'm sure your mother would will want to know what you've been up to in her house."

"My mother?" I asked, pushing up onto my elbows before remembering that I was topless. The blanket slid down, and I flashed poor old Mrs. Grimes a full-frontal of my boobs.

Oops.

Her eyes widened and her mouth puckered into the sourest expression I'd ever seen. "My heavens," she exclaimed, grasping behind her for the doorknob but missing. "Your mother certainly will be interested in this."

"This isn't our mother's house anymore," Waylon growled. "It's our house. And I don't remember inviting you in."

"I can see why," she said in a huff, grabbing the doorknob at last. "And I certainly wouldn't want an invitation now that I know just what goes on in this house."

With that, she yanked open the door, stepped out into the darkness, and slammed the door shut behind her.

"Fuck," Waylon said, taking off his hat and hurling it across the room.

"What should we do?" Holden asked.

"Nothing we can do," Sawyer said. "Did you see her face? There's going to be trouble for sure."

"You'd think she's never heard of a woman falling in a cow trough before," I said indignantly.

"How'd you manage that?" Sawyer asked, a grin starting to spread across his sexy, dark lips.

"The bull chased me in," I said, punching him on the arm. "Don't laugh. I almost died."

"We need to hire you a bodyguard," Waylon said. "It's a full-time job keeping you out of trouble around here."

"The only trouble I see around here is you," I shot back.

"I thought all we had to do was keep you away from cowboys," Sawyer said. "I didn't think we'd have a problem with cows."

"It was a bull," I protested.

"Bullshit it was a bull," Waylon said. "That was straight up heifer."

"Okay, how was I supposed to know?" I asked, throwing up my hands. The blanket slipped again, and this time, all three of them had a fine time ogling my boobs before I pulled it back. I took a deep breath and tried to compose myself and not notice the looks on their faces. "Whatever it was, it outweighs me by about two tons, and it was attacking me."

"She's just being friendly," Sawyer said with a Cheshire grin. "They like to play a little. Tease you a bit. She'd never hurt you."

"You sure you're still talking about the cow?" I asked, looking him up and down.

"And you can tell if it's a heifer because it has udders," Holden said in his low, soft voice, interrupting our moment.

"Okay, okay, I probably should have known that," I admitted. "But still. It wasn't like I was going to crawl under it and see what was hanging down between its legs."

"That's probably smart," Sawyer said, his eyes sparkling with laughter.

"What do we do now?" Holden asked, seating himself beside me on the bearskin rug, his legs stretched out towards the fire.

"I think I should probably get dressed," I said. "In my own clothes."

"Veto," Sawyer said.

"Shut up," I said, pulling the blanket up to my neck.

"You should stay wrapped up," Holden said. "Your body temperature will take a while to go back to normal."

"I wouldn't mind sleeping right here by the fire," I admitted.

"And there's nothing to worry about with nosy old Mrs. Grimes," Sawyer said to Waylon, who was scowling towards the window.

"I should have stopped and talked to her out there," Waylon muttered. "I was trying to get Amber back to the house."

"And you did, and we got her warmed up good," Sawyer said, a knowing smile aimed in my direction.

"Yeah, nothing happened," Holden said. "It might have looked bad, but there was nothing going on."

"You know how she gossips," Waylon said. "She's probably on the phone to our mother right now, and after that, she'll be calling Dad."

"And we'll tell him we're just getting her warmed up," Sawyer said with a grin.

"You better be ready to back up those words, big boy," I said with a sexy smile. "You can't get me warmed up and then leave me hanging."

The smile faltered on his face a bit, and I secretly reveled at the looks flying around the room between the three of them. Did they think I meant it?

Did I?

A blast of wind whipped against the house, whistling across the eaves. I shivered and pulled the blanket tighter around me.

"I'm going to bed," Waylon said, standing abruptly. He was still wearing his long johns, and I tried not to ogle his package through the thin fabric. I couldn't help but notice it was an exceptionally good-sized package. A shiver of longing went through me, and I felt a warmth swelling between my legs, clad only in his pants. If something happened between us, would his brothers find out? Surely our parents never had to.

My eyes climbed his body and met his, and a jolt of connection sizzled through me. I was sure he knew exactly what I'd been thinking. And that he was thinking the exact same thing.

"I'll make sure your mother doesn't find out about this," he said to me. "Because nothing inappropriate happened, and nothing ever will. You're our sister, and that's all you'll ever be to us."

His words were harsh and accusatory, and I felt the rejection like a slap. He knew what I was thinking, all right—but he didn't share those feelings. Instead of reciprocating my feelings, he was reproaching me. My face burned with shame and anger. I knew nothing could happen between us. Just thinking of the humiliation my mother would feel if instead of learning responsibility, I hooked up with my own stepbrothers, made a wave of shame wash over me.

And I sure as hell wasn't going to put myself through having to admit that to her. But here Waylon was, acting like I'd propositioned him. I couldn't help it that I had a wandering eye and an itch that no one had ever scratched.

"Our job is to keep you out of trouble with her, and that's exactly what we're going to do," Sawyer said, his voice not so accusatory, but equally resolved.

I couldn't help but notice that he'd said he would keep me from getting in trouble with her. Not that he'd keep me from doing things she wouldn't approve of. Like being massaged by my three sexy stepbrothers at once, on a bearskin rug in front of a fireplace. While topless.

When Waylon had gone, Holden leaned over and lay a hand over my forehead. "Are you going to be okay?"

"I'm fine," I said, though I didn't know if I'd ever feel warm again. I didn't know if I'd ever felt so frustrated, either. Everything I'd ever wanted was right here in front of me, but I couldn't have any of it. Any of them. I wanted to scream.

"I hope so," Holden said. "Because it's supposed to snow tonight, and sometimes it takes a while to get out after a good snow. You sure you don't need to go see a doctor?"

"We can doctor you up," Sawyer said, smiling down at me. Their two concerned faces hovered over mine, both of theirs rimmed with felt cowboy hats.

"I'm sure you can," I said. "But which one of you gets to be the doctor?"

"I'm the doctor tonight," Sawyer said. "I'm going to sit up with you all night. Make sure you're okay."

"I'm okay," I assured him. "If I need tea or anything, I can make it."

"I told my father I'd look after you," he said. "And I can't sleep on stormy nights, anyway. Consider it a chance to sit up late talking, getting to know your new brother, and being waited on hand and foot." He winked at me, and I felt a thrill of excitement growing inside me. I didn't know how I was going to resist these guys all winter. And worse still, I didn't know which ones I wanted to resist, and which one I wanted to keep. A sneaking suspicion began to dawn inside me. I wasn't falling for one of my hot cowboy step-brothers.

I was falling for all three of them.

Chapter Nineteen

AMBER

AS THE WIND howled outside the large wooden cabin my three stepbrothers owned, I huddled down into the blanket one of them had laid over me after another one had pulled me from a trough of icy cow water. Oh god, I'd fallen in the cow water. I wanted to smack my own forehead. I'd never live this one down.

"You ready for a warm drink?" Sawyer asked, emerging from the kitchen looking sinfully gorgeous in a pair of jeans, a flannel, cowboy boots, and a cowboy hat. I'd never seen him in anything else.

But I wouldn't mind seeing him in a lot less, my shameless mind said.

I nearly groaned out loud. I seriously needed to stop lusting after him, not to mention the other two. If anything happened between any of us… Holden was so sweet I thought I'd ruin him for life, and Waylon was so rough I thought he'd ruin me for life.

And then there was Sawyer, who never stopped flirting long enough for me to think about him the way I should—as a brother.

Carrying a mug in each hand, he lowered himself to the bearskin rug beside me. I sat up, careful to keep the blanket wrapped around myself so I wouldn't flash him. Sawyer handed me a mug of steaming apple cider before hopping up and retrieving all the cushions from the couch. He set them behind me so I had something to lean on, then scooted in beside me, so close our shoulders were pressed against each other.

"To more nights like this," he said, toasting me with his mug. "So we can get to know each other better."

"Minus the near-hypothermic diving lesson," I said, bumping my mug against his. The others had gone to bed, so it was just the two of us, waiting to see how much snow fell outside while we stayed warm and cozy inside.

"I have a question," I said. "If we're getting to know each other."

Sawyer grinned. "Is this like truth or dare?"

"Sort of," I said. "But for now, just truth. Why don't any of you have girlfriends?"

"Who says we don't?"

"You did," I reminded him.

"I said we weren't married."

"So you have a girlfriend?"

"No," he admitted with a grin.

"I asked Holden, but he changed the subject," I said. "So tell me. What's the big secret?"

Sawyer squinted at the fire for a minute, then nodded. "I guess you deserve to know, seeing as how Mrs. Grimes is probably going to make a fuss about what she saw."

"What does that have to do with it?"

"We had a…a woman living here," he said. "For a while. Our grandpa was real excited to have all four of us living in the cabins. He lived in the big house. When he passed, we lived out there still. Waylon brought his woman out here to live in his cabin with him. But one day, she up and ran off with another man. We haven't had another lady living out here since."

"Who's the four of you?" I couldn't help but gulp at the thought of one more irresistible cowboy stepbrother. "Is there another brother I haven't met?"

Sawyer's voice went hard. "And you won't meet him."

"Because he's the one who ran off with Waylon's girlfriend."

Sawyer nodded. "He's been a little jaded about women ever since."

"And what about you?" I asked. "You don't seem jaded. You're as much of a catch as Waylon."

"Why, thank you, ma'am."

"Come on, tell me," I said, leaning over to press my shoulder against his solid one. "I'll tell you my relationship status if you tell me yours."

"We don't get out a lot," he said. "It was hard having a woman around and not having certain thoughts about her. I'm not good at hiding things. She knew it probably before I did. And she flirted with all of us, pitted us against each other. Things were a mess for a while when she left."

"Holden liked her, too?"

Sawyer nodded. "The three of us who were left decided we were brothers first and always would be. Nothing will ever come between us again, not a woman, not money, not anything. We decided then to live here in this house together. There's no jealousy about whose cabin is better, where a woman is sleeping, or who gets more land now that our granddad is gone. We're not splitting the land and each taking a piece. We share everything. We have to agree on everything or it doesn't happen. And that includes bringing a woman here to live. If one of us doesn't like her, if she doesn't get a unanimous vote of approval, we stop seeing her."

"Wow," I said. "That's a lot to expect of a woman. She basically has to meet the standards of all three of you. No wonder you're all single." And e

Even though I wasn't a woman they were interested in, I felt a rising resentment that they had to have such high standards. Good thing I wasn't trying to impress them. If I was, I'd be shit out of luck, because Waylon had to think I was beyond stupid. He probably couldn't wait to get rid of me.

Sawyer shifted and adjusted his jeans, pulling at the knees. It drew my attention straight to his crotch. I could see a bulge in his jeans that made me gulp. "What about you?" he asked. "I told you my story. What's yours?"

I gave him my cheekiest grin. "I'm single," I said, stifling a yawn before snuggling down under the blankets. "Ready to get some sleep?"

Chapter Twenty

AMBER

I WOKE up when Sawyer began to stir. We were lying on the floor, the pillows surrounding us, both under the same blanket. The fire had died down to nothing, and the wind had fallen silent. And something huge and hard was pressed firmly against my ass.

I peeked over my shoulder and saw Sawyer still asleep, his arms cocooning me in their warmth. The decent thing to do would've been to slip out from under the blankets and politely pretend I didn't feel his cock give a throb against my backside. But I'd never been a decent girl.

I wriggled my hips a bit, pushing back into his lap. My god, that thing felt enormous! So enormous that I decided to investigate. I slipped my arm back and slid my hand down between us, my fingers wrapping around his thick shaft. Even through his jeans I could tell he was bigger than anything I'd ever encountered.

He moaned and pressed his hips forward, pressing his cock into my hand. Well, then. Maybe I'd met one brother's standards. I couldn't resist giving him a little squeeze, then running my hand up the length of his cock to the head. I moved it to one side, away from the zipper, and started tracing the outline through his jeans. He groaned again, his arms tightening around me, his hips pushing forward against mine.

I pulled my hand away and arched my back, nestling my ass down into his lap. His breathing went deeper as he pushed back, rocking his hips against mine. I couldn't bear all the clothes between us, so many layers. In that exact position, but naked of course, he'd be ready to slide that enormous cock right into me.

But I heard the shower running upstairs, and footsteps walking across the floor, and I knew the other guys were getting up, too. I didn't want to miss my chance to get to know him in one more way. I could make him forget all about that Maria bitch. And the truth was, I wanted to forget Charlie, too. Now that I knew Sawyer a little, I figured he'd be the guy to help me do just that. He was fun and hot as hell. Out of all the guys, he was the one most likely to overlook the small fact that our parents were married.

"Sawyer?" I whispered. "Should we take this upstairs?"

Sawyer rolled away, his eyes fluttering open. He looked at me like he'd never seen me before. But then his eyes cleared and he smiled. "Amber," he said. "Guess I got you warmed up."

"You have no idea," I said.

He stood and adjusted that huge cock inside his jeans. I couldn't help but stare. And salivate. With a grin, Sawyer leaned down to pat my hip. "You got me warm, too," he said with a grin. "I better go take a shower."

Without another word, he turned and trotted up the stairs.

I rolled onto my back and groaned, throwing my arm over my eyes. It was still dark out, which meant there was no earthly reason for me to be awake. Except that I was horny as fuck and surrounded by three hot as hell cowboys who were off limits. I groaned again.

"You okay there, Princess?"

I uncovered my eyes to see Waylon standing over me with a smirk on his face.

"I don't know, Cowboy," I said, standing with my back to him and dropping the blanket from my shoulders. My hair fell in tangles down my back, but I turned and gave him a meaningful look over my shoulder. "Am I?"

His face was blank and hard. "I'd like those back when you're done with them," he said, nodding at his pants.

"I'm done with them," I said. They were sliding down my hips anyway. I just gave them a little help, hooking my fingers in the band and pulling them slowly down to my ankles, bending over as I did so. I stepped out of them, gathered them up, and turned to give them to Waylon. His face remained hard, his eyes black as midnight, his jaw clenched. I strolled over, picked up his hand, and pushed the pants into it. "Thanks for taking such good care of me," I said, standing on tiptoes to brush a kiss across his cheek.

I darted up the stairs, a hysterical giggle building in my throat. I couldn't believe I'd just done that! I blamed it on Sawyer for leaving me horny and the darkness for making me bold. It always seemed like whatever happened after dark didn't count, that it wasn't me. I could take too many shots of tequila or get sick out the door of a cab or make out with a club owner I'd never met. I could sneak a pint of ice cream out of the freezer and eat the entire thing while watching reruns of *Community* in worn-out sweatpants. If it happened in the dark, it seemed detached from the person I was in daylight.

At the top of the stairs, I took two steps and ran into a

wall—a hot, steamy wall of muscle. I shrieked in surprise at the full-body collision, every inch of my bare skin connecting with every inch of his. Bouncing off, I did my best to steady myself while Holden gaped openly at me. The hallway was dark, lit only by one bedroom door standing open behind me. But once my eyes adjusted, I could see that he was stark naked, too. Steam curled up from his skin, still damp from a hot shower.

"I'm sorry," he stammered.

"Wow," I blurted out. I'd never seen so much skin, and it was glorious. Every muscle in his body was well-defined and bulging. Chill bumps covered his skin from the chilly air in the hallway, and his dark nipples were hard. I'd never wanted to touch something so bad in my life. Before I could think up a good excuse, I reached up and ran my fingers across the expanse of one of his massive pecs. My fingertips grazed one of his erect nipples, and we both sucked in a breath at the same time.

My eyes traveled down his sculpted torso, his narrow hips, to the dark patch of hair around his cock, which had begun to stir. I couldn't tell for sure, but once it was hard, it might be even bigger than Sawyer's. I gasped at the thought, biting my lip as my eyes returned to his. A long, silent moment passed.

"I was just going—" I broke off, gesturing to my room behind him.

"Me, too," he said, his eyes fixed on the open bedroom door behind me. "I just got out of the shower, and…" He stopped speaking, his throat working as his eyes drank me in like a man dying of thirst, finally quenched.

"I better go," I said, edging around him. He flattened himself against the wall, as if frightened we might accidentally touch as we eased past each other. As soon as we'd switched places, I dashed to my room. Closing the door, I dove onto my bed, stifling a shriek in my pillow. I'd never been so humiliated, and excited, and giddy at once, and I just couldn't contain it. Sometimes, you have to scream it out.

At last, I rolled over, grabbed my phone, and texted Haley. "Call me asap."

The next minute, my phone rang. "What happened?" she demanded in lieu of a hello.

"I just ran into Holden," I said. "Naked."

"You do live together," Haley said. "And they're guys. My brother still runs around naked sometimes."

"Your brother is an animal."

"Okay, true," she said. "But they just don't know how to live with a girl anymore. They probably trot around naked all the time when you're not there."

I swallowed hard at the thought of them all walking around naked. Together. Oh God. I was seriously in deep.

"I was naked, too," I admitted.

"You were not!" Haley squealed.

"I was," I said, covering my face. "I ran upstairs naked, and he was getting out of the shower, and boom. Full-frontal connection."

"Can I trade lives with you?" Haley sighed.

"Wait, why are you even up?" I asked, pulling my phone away from my ear to look at it. It was four-thirty in the morning. "Are you out partying?"

Haley yawned loudly. "No, I'm binge-watching *Supernatural.*"

"I'm jealous."

"Shut up, you have hot cowboys traipsing around naked in your house."

"Who I can't have," I reminded her.

"I'll take them," she said. "All three of them."

"Preferably at once," I said with a shiver.

"Amber," she said, sounding scandalized. "You're supposed to be in Wyoming to get your ducks in a row, not to get your dicks in a row."

"Oh, I don't want them in a row," I said, rolling onto my back and pulling the blankets up over me. "I want them in a circle."

Chapter Twenty-One

WAYLON

THE TABLE WAS silent as we all sat down to eat breakfast. Finally, I couldn't take it. That bastard was holding out on us.

"You gonna make me ask?" I growled at my brother.

Sawyer smiled, finishing his mouthful of eggs before answering. "Nah," he said. "Not that. Just trying to put off the inevitable because I know you're going to be pissed."

"Did something happen?" Holden asked, not looking up from his plate.

I watched him as Sawyer spoke, though. When that cheating bitch had run off on me, I'd been fine. Holden had taken it hardest. He was the reason I'd shot down the women they'd brought home since then. But it was harder now. I couldn't simply find a reason to send Amber home, though God knew she had made enough messes. I had blown off other women for far less legitimate reasons. But despite Amber's mishaps, I couldn't send her packing. She was here for two and a half more months, like it or not.

"I told her about Maria," Sawyer said. "I didn't mean to, not really. We got to talking, and she's easy to talk to."

"Dangerously easy," Holden said. "You're going to scare her off."

"It doesn't matter," I reminded them. "She's not a woman."

"She sure looks like a woman to me," Holden said.

A picture of her bending over with her ass in the air flashed through my mind, and my cock throbbed painfully hard. It did not agree with my brain on this one.

"I like her," Sawyer said. "I think we should feel her out."

"She's our sister," I reminded him.

"We're all adults, and our parents happened to get married," Sawyer said. "She's not our sister."

"I like her, too," Holden said quietly. "And there's nothing sisterly about her. I say yes."

I'd been afraid of that.

"We all know we need a woman around," Sawyer said. "And she's already here. She seems to like us all, right? This is what we need. Someone who won't come between us because we're all there for her. She doesn't have to hide it or run off with one of us. She gets all of us. And we get her."

"That all sounds good to me," Holden said. "Who cares what anyone else thinks? This is between us and her. No one else needs to know."

"And if they find out, fuck them," Sawyer said. "The only thing that matters is that she's happy with it."

"No," I said firmly. "I like her as much as you do. Trust me, I do. But regardless of what we need, we have to put what she needs first. And the last thing she needs is more scandal. She came here to get away from that."

"If we keep it quiet, there won't be a scandal," Sawyer said.

"But they will find out," I said. "You saw how easy it

was last night. You know what they'd say about her if they got wind of it. The senator's daughter is living in sin with three men? Not to mention, her own stepbrothers?"

"You're right," Holden said. "They'd crucify her. The gossip about her arrest would be nothing compared to this."

"If we're not in agreement, then it doesn't happen," Sawyer said. "But I think you're making a mistake."

The picture of Amber flashed in my mind again, the look she cast me over her bare shoulder, how she bent all the way down to her toes so I could see every inch of her. I couldn't help but wonder if he was right. But we couldn't risk her reputation, no matter what we needed.

"Then it won't happen," I said. The legs of my chair scraped across the floor as I stood. "Do whatever you need to do to stop thinking about her."

Chapter Twenty-Two

AMBER

I NEEDED TO GET LAID. Instead, I was locked up in a house that was a hundred times worse than a convent. In a convent, I'd be around a bunch of other women, and we'd all be covered head to toe so no naughty thoughts could enter our minds. Here, all I had were naughty thoughts. Could you blame me? I was locked up with three irresistible men who were intent on resisting me, if the next week was any indication.

I hadn't seen so much as a chink in Waylon's armor. He'd been especially surly when I mentioned all the tourists I'd seen heading up towards the ski areas.

"I'm just trying to help," I said lightly, letting my gaze stray towards the empty cabins behind the house.

Even Sawyer met my attempts to flirt with stoic indifference.

The snow remained on the ground, a good foot of it. Instead of turning grey and being pushed into huge sooty mountains, as it was in New York, it remained pure white here. The first day, it blew in swirls across the fields, but after that, a sparkly crust developed on top of it. For the first time in my life, I understood where the term *winter wonderland* came from.

And it wasn't from *wondering* when the slush would stop ruining my boots.

I went out walking every day, trying to cure my blues. I helped with meals and taking care of the house. While the guys were out, I read and looked at Pinterest for decorating ideas, so I could spruce up the house. Maybe I was only going to be there a couple more months, but it wouldn't hurt the house to look a little more welcoming and less like a bachelor pad. At least they didn't have calendars with naked girls or beer signs hanging around.

I even started ordering things to decorate. I called Haley every day. But it was lonely as fuck, if I was honest. Despair started to pull me down like quicksand no matter how many times I told myself I was only there for three months, and that their rejection was warranted and not thrice the equivalent of Charlie's.

After all, Charlie had wanted me back. I'd finally fought through the haze of that night and recovered at least some of the memories I'd blacked out.

We'd gone out dancing, and as Haley's brother predicted, I'd ended up schnockered. A large, sweaty man in too-tight pants was buying me drinks, which I happily accepted.

"I told you I was going to get laid," I bellowed in Haley's ear, draping my arms around her neck as I stumbled against her on the dance floor.

"Um, I'm going to have to veto your choice of devirgination devices," she said. "That guy has date rapist written all over him."

"But I want him," I moaned. "So it's not rape."

"You don't want him, you want to forget Charlie, and

you're hammered," she said. "So hammered that they're going to kick us out if I don't cut you off soon."

"I'm not that drunk," I screamed. "I can still stand on one leg!" And with that, I proceeded to demonstrate by pulling my leg straight up—thanks for those ballet classes, Mom—and hook my foot behind my head. And then I fell flat on my ass.

A minute later, as predicted, the bouncers asked us to leave. "We should go find Charlie," I said as I swerved out the door onto the sidewalk.

"You hate Charlie, remember?"

"Oh, right," I said. "But maybe now that I caught him hooking up with another girl, he won't have an excuse not to hook up with me."

A transvestite hooker was standing outside smoking a cigarette, wearing a bandage-sized skirt and red heels even though it was October. "Oh, honey, that's just sad," she said, giving me a pitying look.

Haley and I started giggling madly, until the hooker moved further off down the street, casting us disparaging glances.

"But I know him, and I love him," I said as I fell into a cab with Haley. "Shouldn't he be the one I give it up to?"

"Shut up or I will hit you," she said. "The only thing you're giving to him is more soup burns."

The cabbie dumped us off at Haley's, and we ran up to her flat, making way more noise than was necessary. Mark stepped out of the kitchen wearing his boxer shorts, a carton of Chinese food in one hand. "Hey, look, it's my sister and her drunk friend," he said.

"Go die in a hole," I said, heading for Haley's room.

"Charlie called me," Mark said behind me. I turned to see him leaning on against the island in the kitchen, digging through his food with a pair of chopsticks.

"What'd he say?" I asked, a ridiculous lurch in my stomach. I was pretty sure it was nerves, not the desire to puke, but I couldn't be certain. I'd taken a lot of shots.

"Oh, just that you weren't answering your phone," Mark said.

I grabbed for my purse, rummaging for my phone, but before I could find it, Haley wrenched it from my hand and dashed into her room. I stumbled after her, protesting all the way.

"Just let me see what he said," I said, grabbing for my phone, which she had extracted from my purse.

She thumbed through my texts. "He said…blah blah blah, bullshit bullshit bullshit, lies lies lies."

"What did he really say?"

"He's worried about you and wants to talk. I guess not too worried to stop getting a blowjob, though. Notice how he waited until he came to start texting."

"You're right," I said, taking my phone. "I'm erasing his number…right after I text him."

We were still wrestling over the phone when Mark stepped into the room, still munching on his Chinese. "That would be hot if one of you wasn't my sister," he said, holding up his phone to snap a picture. "I'll send this to Charlie, tell him he turned you into a lesbian."

We thought he was kidding, but fifteen minutes later, Charlie texted to say he was outside. Haley threw open her window, which overlooked the street. "Amber says to eat shit and die," she yelled.

"I just want to talk," he yelled back. "Amber, just hear me out."

"What?" I said, sticking my head out the window next to Haley. I cupped my hand around one ear and leaned out further. "I can't hear you. It sounds like you're talking through a mouthful of pussy."

"Come down and talk," he yelled. "Please?"

Someone yelled at us to shut up, but I didn't care. It was like a hole had been blown in my chest, and it was full of pain and anger and vengeance. And tequila. But the point is, I wanted him to hurt like I was hurting.

"Do you have any soup?" I asked Haley. "We could stick it in the microwave."

"I have something better," she said.

While Charlie howled for us to come back, we ran to the fridge to get the two dozen eggs she had there.

"Psycho," Mark muttered. "I'm getting out of here."

He went to his room, and we went to the window.

To be honest, I don't think I hit Charlie with a single egg. My hand-eye coordination was not its best. But Haley had played softball for a while, and her aim was much more accurate. So I handed her eggs, and she threw, and Charlie swore at us.

And then the cops showed up.

Chapter Twenty-Three

AMBER

AFTER A WEEK of weirdness with my stepbrothers, I couldn't take it anymore. One night when the guys had gone to bed, I was creeping along the hall to the bathroom, careful to step lightly so I wouldn't wake them, when I saw a light on under Holden's door. He'd been the least weird to me since I'd hit on pretty much all three of them, so I figured it was my best shot. I gathered my courage and tapped on his door.

I heard him murmur something, so I pushed open the door. He looked up from where he was sitting at an easel, and his eyes went wide with shock. He jumped up, his big thigh knocking into his canvas, which went crashing to the floor, along with tubes of paint and brushes.

"Oh, sorry," I said, flustered by the chaos. "I didn't mean to startle you. I thought I heard you tell me to come in, but maybe you were just talking to yourself. No judgement, I mean, I talk to myself all the time."

"It's okay," Holden said. He'd grabbed up the canvas and replaced it on the easel, but not before I saw enough to know he was painting a naked blonde girl.

"I didn't know you painted," I said, relaxing a little. I knelt to help him gather up the tubes of oil paints.

"Yeah," he said, not looking at me. I was pretty sure he was blushing.

"That's really cool," I said.

"Uh huh."

"I mean it," I said, putting my hand on his. He paused in his frantic gathering and stared at our hands. "I mean, I wouldn't expect a cowboy to be a painter, too. But that's a good thing, not a bad thing."

He swallowed, still staring at our hands. "I got a lot of shit for it growing up around here," he said quietly. "Guys around here pride themselves on being tough. Not painting."

"Well, I think it's sexy," I said. "It makes you…unpredictable. There's more to you than meets the eye."

"I don't know about that," Holden said. "I'm pretty much what-you-see-is-what-you-get."

"Nothing wrong with that," I said, admiring his arms, clad in a t-shirt. He was wearing light blue flannel pajama pants with little horseshoes on them.

He looked slightly embarrassed when he noticed me studying them. "Our ma," he said.

"Could you be any cuter?" I blurted out before I could stop myself.

Holden finished gathering all the paints into his two giant paws and replaced them in the empty coffee canister that they'd spilled from.

"So uh…what'd you stop in for?" he asked, scratching his head and settling his huge frame onto the tiny stool in front of the easel.

"Can I see it?" I asked, nodding towards the canvas.

His face turned red and he shifted uncomfortably. "I usually don't show people until they're done," he said.

I gave him a sly smile. "Even your model?"

If it was possible, his face got even redder. "I—I didn't think you saw it," he stammered.

"I saw a little," I admitted, slipping across the room to stand beside him.

The painting wasn't exactly beautiful. I didn't think it would be displayed at the MET anytime soon, but it had a certain appeal. The kind of appeal that calendars with scantily clad women had.

The woman in the painting was definitely me. I thought. She had long blonde hair falling around her shoulders to her waist, long legs that were a couple shades paler than mine, and boobs that were maybe a bit exaggerated. Okay, more than a bit. A couple cup sizes. He'd put a bit of a fantasy spin on me, if I was honest. There were no problem areas on that painting.

The woman wore nothing but a cowboy hat held over her lady parts with one hand. Her other hand was held up like she was covering her mouth, which was a little red O of surprise. Her eyes were wide with shock. It was a pretty way to portray my shame that day in the hall, when I'd run into him naked.

Behind the naked woman was a pastel, prairie landscape, which brought into contrast her milky white skin and bright pink nipples.

"Oh, wow," I said after a minute. "That's…interesting."

To my surprise, instead of getting embarrassed, Holden chuckled. "Don't worry," he said. "I usually sell them, but I might keep this one."

"Is there a market for this kind of thing?" I asked, then winced at the incredulous note in my voice.

"You'd be surprised," Holden said.

"Well, it's not the direction I was going to go with decorating the place, but…"

"That's all right," he said quickly. "We don't put them around the house."

"Do you have any others here?" I asked, glancing around his room. Like the rest of the house, it was completely devoid of decoration or personality.

"I have a batch in the closet," he said, standing and moving to open the door. I followed and pulled them out, studying them one by one. A buxom redhead in a Betty Boop pose wearing only a cowboy hat and boots, in the desert. A dark-haired, exotic beauty standing on the far side of a wooden fence, the rails strategically hiding certain areas. A blonde wearing nothing but leather chaps, looking back over her shoulder. Another dark-haired exotic beauty riding a horse.

"Now that doesn't look very comfortable," I said.

Holden shuffled his feet. "It's just a painting."

"I know, I'm kidding," I said, giving his shoulder a playful shove. "So are these all the girls you've seen naked lately?"

He rubbed the back of his neck. "Not really."

I laughed and lifted another canvas. "Maria?" I asked, holding up yet another of the dark-haired woman standing beneath a stormy sky.

He swallowed before giving a curt nod.

"It's okay," I said, setting down the painting and touching his elbow. "Sawyer told me about her."

"I know."

I pulled back in surprise. "You do?"

"We share everything," he said with a shrug.

"Everything?" I asked with a meaningful look at the paintings.

"They know I paint," he said. "We've lived together all our lives."

He was so innocent I didn't want to spoil it by telling him what I really meant. After all, that's how I'd gotten into this whole awkward situation with them.

"So this bitch who broke your heart," I said, sitting down and gesturing to the painting. "Can I hunt her down and kick her ass?"

Chapter Twenty-Four

AMBER

BEFORE HOLDEN COULD RESPOND, his phone rang. He checked it before shutting off the ringer and setting it back on his bedside table. I was glad he hadn't used the phone call as an excuse to get out of answering my question, but I couldn't help but wonder if it was a woman calling, and that's why he hadn't answered. A little flare of protectiveness rose in me. If I had anything to do with it, I'd be joining in on their application process for future lady friends. Not just anyone was good enough for my gentle giant of a stepbrother.

"So about this Maria," I said, gesturing to a painting. "Do you know where she is now?"

"No," Holden said with a shrug, staring at the picture. "We haven't talked to either of them since they took off. That was three years ago."

"And you're all still hung up on her?" I could barely remember my boyfriend from three years ago, the one before Charlie.

"It's not like that," he said. "We're not in love with her anymore. It just taught us to be careful with who we trust."

"Well, thank you for trusting me enough to tell me," I said, touching his arm again. "And to show me your paintings."

"You're our sister," he said with a shrug.

Both of us turned to the painting on the easel at the same moment. "We're not related," I reminded him. "Not by blood."

"I know," he said. "But most people don't make that distinction."

"I think they do," I said, my hand lingering on his arm. God, I wanted to feel up that muscle. I must be getting really desperate if I was fantasizing about groping his arm. And feeling them wrapped tight around me, crushing me under that barrel chest of his…

"You saw Mrs. Grimes last week," he said.

"I hope she never sees these paintings," I said, trying to lighten the mood.

Holden smiled. "Lord help us if she does."

"Yeah," I said. "I actually came in here to ask about that. And to say I'm sorry."

"For what?"

"For the other day," I said. "When we ran into each other. I don't want things to be awkward anymore. I've been so bored and lonely since you stopped talking to me." I didn't mention that I'd been so lonely I'd almost broken down and called Charlie. I had lots of time to think about him while my stepbrothers were ignoring me.

A pained expression crossed Holden's face. "Shit, I'm sorry," he said. "You're right, we've been rude. I didn't think how…" He broke off and shook his head. "You're alone here, and we've got each other."

"I know I'm not part of your boys' club," I said. "And I'm okay with that. I'm not a guy, and I totally messed up the other day and crossed all kinds of boundaries you have with women. But if you could hold off on unanimously deciding I'm a hopeless case for like two more months, I'd so appreciate that."

Holden smiled and hooked his arm around my neck, pulling me close. "You're not a hopeless case," he said, kissing my forehead.

It should have been a totally brotherly hug, and I should have pulled away and socked him in the arm, but oh… He smelled like clean laundry and hay, and my cheek pressed against his solid pecs, and my hands found his hips. Every part of him was just so big! My hands felt tiny on his body. And instead of letting me go, he kept his arm around me, and his nose pressed into my hair for a second. I closed my eyes and sighed, melting against him.

"Amber," he said, his quiet voice choked.

"Mmm?"

His arm slid down from around the back of my neck, down my shoulders, my back. It settled around my waist, pulling me hard against him. Through his thin pajamas and my long-sleeved tee, I could feel his cock beginning to harden against my belly. His knees bent a little, and he stooped to kiss the side of my head, nuzzling my hair.

It was automatic, I swear it. But I lifted my face to his without even thinking. Of course I knew it was wrong to be kissing my stepbrother, but I couldn't help myself. He was so sexy, and he smelled so good, and he felt so good pressed up against me…

My lips yearned for his, and when they found them, they never wanted to stop. To be honest, I wanted a lot more than a kiss. My thighs quaked at the sensation of his hardness pressed against me. I wanted to feel more of that. But despite that rigid, ramrod cock, his lips were soft as velvet against mine, his kiss as soft and gentle as I would have imagined if I'd ever imagined kissing him. Which I totally hadn't.

His arm tightened around me, crushing me against his body, but his lips remained soft and careful. As his other hand stroked my hair, I dug my own hands into his brown hair, standing on tiptoes and pressing into the kiss. A long, passionate sigh escaped him. Together, our lips found a slow, steady rhythm that made heat spread through my body, settling at last between my thighs.

The wind rattled outside the house. An owl hooted somewhere nearby. Far away, a pack of coyotes sang. Holden's arms held me close, bending my body back slightly as he held it against his. Though I could feel his excitement growing against me, he didn't rub it against me or change his hold. He just kissed me tenderly, warmly, continuously, until my lips felt swollen and my whole body was on fire. I thought I'd explode if we didn't move to the bed soon.

Instead, Holden slowly pulled away. He cupped my cheek in his hand, his eyes swimming with adoration and awe.

"Amber," he said, his voice dreamy and slightly rough. The way he said my name made me shiver with longing, as if my name itself were a precious treasure.

"Yes?" I breathed.

And then he said the words I wished he'd never say. "We can't."

"I know," I said, sinking down from my tiptoes.

With a pained expression, he gave me one last squeeze before letting me go. "I'm sorry," he said, but I didn't know if he was apologizing that we couldn't go any further or for the kiss. Somehow, I didn't think this would help with the issue of things being super awkward because we were related and madly attracted to each other.

"Me, too," I said. "But it's probably for the best. I

mean, I won't lie, you're hot as hell. But I'm just too confused by all this to do anything, anyway."

His brow creased with concern. "What are you confused by? Let me help."

"You'd think I was a slut."

"I'd never think that," he said, his eyebrows drawing into a frown.

"Here's the thing. I think you're like the sweetest guy I've ever met, and super-hot to boot, but…well, I also kind of think your brothers are pretty awesome, and I may have had a moment with one or both of them last week. The same morning we ran into each other. Does that make me a terrible human being?"

Holden took my hand and pulled me close, brushing my hair back again. "It doesn't make you a terrible human being," he said, kissing me softly.

"Seriously? You don't care?"

"I care about you," he said. "And I care about my brothers. I want you to be happy, and I want them to be happy."

I swallowed hard. How could he be so accepting?

"What does that mean?" I whispered. "You'd be okay only having a third of my heart?"

"As long as together, we have all of you," Holden said, his eyes earnest. "I don't think of it as measuring off pieces of you. I want all of you, every bit of you, body and soul and heart and everything else. But I want it for all of us. My brother's happiness is as important to me as my own."

"That's generous of you," I said, thinking of Waylon's possessive, hard eyes. "But I don't know if the others would agree."

"I do," he said fiercely. "But what's even more important to me than our happiness is yours."

I swallowed hard, feeling oddly naked. Was this what

vulnerability felt like? I'd been too mad and hurt by Charlie to feel this way. But this time, I was standing before the man rejecting me. It was terrifying, and it kind of sucked.

"What do you want, Amber?" Holden asked, holding me firmly even when I started to pull away. "What would make you happy?"

"I don't know," I said. I had the sudden urge to run away and hide. This was too much, too fast. He looked like he freaking loved me. And I had to pick right now? How could I not pick him? He was adorable and good and sweet and oh God, I could just imagine how generous he would be in bed. But then there was Sawyer, who would build pillow forts with me and tickle me and chase me around the bedroom. And Waylon…a shiver of excitement tinged with fear ran through me when I thought of what he would be like between the sheets.

But I'd just broken up with my boyfriend of three years. It hadn't even been a month. What if this was just lust, just a rebound? What if I was subconsciously doing it go get back at him? That wasn't fair to the guys. And then there was the little matter of my inexperience. They'd want a real woman, one who could keep up. Not a virgin.

"If it's just one of us, and it's not me, I'll be just as happy for both of you," Holden said. "But if it's all of us, that's what you'll get."

"I—I can't choose right now," I said. "I'm so sorry."

Suddenly, tears threatened, and I had to get out of there. Holden's voice echoed in my ears even after I'd stepped out into the hall and hurried back to my room.

"You don't have to."

Did he mean I didn't have to choose right now? Or I didn't have to choose at all?

Thank you for reading!
If you'd like more of this series,
make sure to leave a review letting me know.

Don't miss book 2 in the series, coming soon.

Keep reading for an exclusive
sneak peek at Book 2, *Wrangle Me, Cowboys.*

More from Alexa

Wrangle Me, Cowboys

Excerpt of Coyote Ranch, Book 2

Chapter 1

THE MORNING after I kissed my stepbrother, I woke up to the bright light of a Wyoming morning. The room was a bit chilly, but I snuggled down under the comforter and smiled to myself, remembering that kiss. Remembering the sensation of Holden's huge, muscular body pressing against mine. Remembering his cock hardening against me.

I rolled over and pulled open the drawer of the nightstand, reaching for my vibrator. I'd gotten used to being sexually frustrated after three years of dating a hold-out who turned out to be a cheating piece of shit who was only holding out on me.

To my even greater frustration, as my hand brushed the bottom of the empty drawer, I realized I'd left my vibrator back in New York. After all, I'd thought I was coming here to babysit, not fall into paroxysms of lust over three sexy cowboys. With a groan, I fell back on my pillow, my arm across my eyes. What a craptastic way to ruin the good feeling I'd had when I woke.

On the nightstand, my phone buzzed, taunting me.

I picked it up and looked at it, an idea forming in my mind. My phone vibrated....

Five minutes later, I called my best friend Haley back. "I need an intervention," I blurted when she answered.

"Aww, Amber. Are you drinking yourself into a coma every night thinking of how much you miss me?"

"I do miss you," I said. "But no. I'm pretty sure I just violated my phone in ways no one has ever done before. I can't even believe I'm holding it against my face right now."

"Did you put it *inside* your underwear?" Haley asked.

"What? How did you even know what I was talking about?"

"Emergency vibe," she said, as if it were obvious.

I tried not to think about how many times I'd used her phone.

"So, did you?" she asked. "Because yeah, that's like sexual assault of a mobile device. But otherwise, you're good."

"Then I'm good," I said, relieved that I wasn't the first woman to get desperate enough to hump her iPhone.

"And hey, no pussy juice on your face," Haley added.

"Did you just call it pussy juice?"

"Well, I could have said come, but you'd probably enjoy getting come on your face."

"You'd know."

"It's like a warm facial," she said. "But seriously, Am. Just go buy a vibrator."

"There are no cabs here," I said. "No buses. No subway. Basically, I'm trapped and at the mercy of my stepbrothers."

"Ahhh," she said. "So that's why you need to masturbate with your phone. The sexy stepbrother. Which one are you lusting after this time?"

"All of them," I wailed. "I can't decide. And honestly, Haley, I don't think they want me to."

"Ugh, don't tell me they're putting you in a nunnery like the Threesome King."

That was the name Haley had given my ex after we walked in on him having a threesome. For years, I'd let him know I'd be open to sex or other things, but he'd been insistent on preserving my virginity. Like it was something to put in a freaking museum.

"I'm not sure," I said. "They definitely aren't trying to shut me up in a nunnery, but we are related…"

"Uh…no? To be related, they'd have to be your actual brothers."

"So you'd be cool sleeping with your stepbrothers?"

"Ew, no, because they're little kids and I was there when they were born," Haley said. "You just met these guys. And if they want you and you want them… No judgment."

"But there's three of them. What if they get jealous and weird?"

"So they all want you, together, at the same time?"

"I think so," I squeaked.

"Well, I guess you won the breakup. A foursome beats a threesome."

"Four mouths are better than three," I said, paraphrasing the evil ex, and we both dissolved into laughter.

But I did wonder. Holden had told me I didn't have to choose. Maybe he hadn't meant it the way I'd taken it. Maybe he'd meant it like, I didn't have to worry about choosing because they would never hook up with their stepsister, no matter how perfect that kiss had been.

But I didn't think so. I thought he meant it like, I didn't have to choose because I could have them all. Which just seemed too good to be true, and also, I worried about the logistics of it. Would I rotate from one room to the next each night? Would we need to make a schedule? What if I needed a night off or I had my period? What if one of them got mad because I made more noise in the room next door with his brother? What if I just wanted to be held by big, cuddly Holden, but it was rough-and-ready Waylon's night?

Or would it be a foursome—all three of them at the same time? And if it was that, could I handle it?

Chapter 2

A WHILE LATER, I'd when I'd calmed down, I saw Waylon heading for the shop out beyond the five empty cabins behind the house. I threw together a sandwich as an excuse and let myself out the back door. I wasn't sure if Holden had told his brothers about our kiss, or if I should tell them first. I didn't know how this whole thing worked at all, but I knew they didn't like secrets. If I came clean about it, I figured they'd respect me. Then again, it might get Holden in trouble.

Either way, I wanted to feel Waylon out, see how he felt about it and find out if he knew. So I balanced the plate and headed out. I'd never been inside the shop, though I'd seen the guys pulling their farm equipment in and out of it. This seemed like a good time to go explore. When I stepped inside, it was a bit gloomy, despite the overhead fluorescents. It took a minute for my eyes to adjust. The huge tractor was up front, the one that Waylon had driven out to pull me from the cow trough on the night of the infamous topless massage.

Hurrying between that and the side-by-side, I spotted

movement at the back of the shop. I hurried back and found Waylon halfway under the hood of an orange muscle car. He had his usual tan Carhartt coveralls on, but the top was peeled down to hang around his waist like jeans. His white t-shirt showed off his lean muscles. For a minute, I stood there watching him turn a wrench, wondering if it was possible he could be any hotter.

"I brought you a sandwich," I said at last.

Waylon straightened up so fast his head hit the bottom of the hood, and his cowboy hat toppled off, landing in the engine. He growled a curse and plucked it up, replacing it on his head as he turned to me.

"What'd you need?" he asked.

"I…" I trailed off, stung by his short response. I should have been used to it by then. Waylon wasn't a man of many words, and when he did use words, they weren't especially pleasant ones. I tried to imagine what he'd been like with Maria, the ex who had run off and left him for his brother.

"Is that for me?" he asked, plucking the sandwich from the plate. He took a big bite of it and then stood chewing and looking down at it. "What's that taste?"

"It's avocado mayo," I said. "Made with truffle oil."

"Huh." He took another bite.

"Do you like it?" I asked hopefully.

"What's wrong with regular mayo?" he asked, depositing the half-eaten sandwich before turning back to his car.

But I could not be dissuaded that easily. I'd wear him down eventually. No matter how surly he was, I could always get a smile out of him. I sidled up to the car and leaned against it. "So you fix cars?"

"I'm rebuilding the engine," he said, not looking up from his tools.

I tried to pose sexily against the car, but I immediately started sliding back along it. Seriously, looking sexy was a bit difficult while balancing a plate on one hand. I mean, the car was really polished!

"Don't scuff the wax," Waylon said from under the hood.

I propped myself against the side mirror and nibbled at his sandwich. "Did Holden tell you what happened last night?" I asked.

"What happened?" he asked, not sounding interested at all.

"We kissed."

"Is that right," he said flatly.

"He said you were all okay with…us being together. All four of us. So I guess I'm just wondering…how does it work?"

Finally, Waylon picked up a rag and wiped his hands roughly on it. "It doesn't," he said shortly. "My father's lending us money to save the ranch if we keep you out of trouble for the next two months. That's all."

"He's paying you?" I asked incredulously.

Waylon paused, guilt flickering across his face. "Lending us money," he said after a few seconds. "Not giving it to us."

"So you're babysitting me?" I asked, humiliating building.

"Call it what you like," Waylon said. "You knew we were doing our parents a favor by taking you in."

"I didn't know you were getting *paid*," I said. "I thought we were supposed to get to know our new family a little. That I'd come out here and help out, and you'd let me stay."

"That's what's happening, isn't it?"

"I didn't realize I was such a pain the ass that you had to get paid to get to know me."

"You're a royal pain in the ass, Princess," he said, stepping around the open hood of the car. He had a grease smear on his bare, tan arm. I wanted to freaking lick it. How had I fallen so hard for someone who had to get a paycheck to spend time with me?

But hell, if they were my gigolos, shouldn't I be getting more action?

Waylon took the sandwich from me and took a bite before handing it back. "I didn't ask for money," he said. "I didn't ask for you to come stay here. Our father offered us a deal. Keep you out of trouble, and he'd lend us some money to help keep the ranch going. That's all."

"I just wish I'd known to begin with," I said. "I thought you were all so keen on honesty and openness and not keeping secrets."

"From each other," he said.

His words stung, though I tried to hide it. I wasn't one of them. They were a family who looked out for each other, trusted each other, cared about each other. And I was their stepmother's daughter.

"Well, thanks for telling me," I said.

"Amber," he said, his voice gruff. "What happened with Holden shouldn't have happened. He's my brother, but I'll be the first to admit, he's got a weakness when it comes to good-looking women."

"So you think I'm good looking," I teased.

"What do you want me to say?" he asked. "If you weren't my stepsister, I'd bend you over the hood of this car and fuck you until you screamed loud enough for every neighbor in the next ten miles to come see who was making such a fuss?"

"Oh," I whispered, my thighs quaking at that image.

"That doesn't change the fact that you are my stepsister." He finished the sandwich and picked up the grease rag to wipe his hands again. "Keeping an eye on you means keeping you out of trouble in town, or with the law, but it also means protecting you. Out here, the rules are a little different than what you're used to in New York."

"So you've said. But they don't seem so different to me."

"People see something they want, they take it," he said. "Ranchers came out here to claim land. There's a little of that spirit left."

"Good to know," I said. "I guess you haven't seen anything you wanted in three years?"

His mouth twisted into a smirk. "Sometimes we want something for a night," he said. "But nothing we've wanted to keep."

I took that as a challenge.

Coyote Ranch, Book two coming soon.

Coming Soon

Coyote Ranch, Book Two

www.ingramcontent.com/pod-product-compliance
Lightning Source LLC
Chambersburg PA
CBHW020407130626
46549CB00006B/2470